Whistler's
NIGHT

USA TODAY BESTSELLING AUTHOR
H.M. SHANDER

Kathy
happy holidays!

Best
Shander

Whistler's Night
Published by H.M. Shander
Copyright 2021 H.M. Shander

Cover Design: Francessca Wingfield @ Francessca's PR & Designs
Editing: PWA & IDIM Editorial
Shander, H.M., 1975—Whistler's Night

If you ever get the opportunity

for a second chance, take it!

Chapter

ONE

Parking my car in the far corner of the lot, I exited with my coveted tram ticket in hand, and stared up to the peak. The building at the summit, some 2300 feet above sea level, sat like a dark smudge against the green tops of the evergreens on the side of Whistler's Mountain. I couldn't wait to get up there and put some perspective on my life. I needed a clear place to think, and nothing else in the area screamed peaceful like that.

Besides, today was my twenty-eighth birthday and way back when I was a kid, I had dreams. Big dreams. Until they all crashed and burned several years ago. Deep down in my soul, something told me it was time to stop living in the past and to take the first steps forward. Starting today.

Maybe it was the birthday gift I'd purchased for myself – a visit with a psychic – that spurred me on. I knew it was all in fun, and that their predictions for the future were general at best, but still. Her words hit me like a bolt to the heart; how it was going to be a monumental weekend, with new life, and how tonight specifically would be my undoing and a chance to start fresh.

I'd kept my snicker contained and secretly rolled my eyes. Of course tonight was going to be *my undoing and a chance to start fresh* - I was going to inform Noah, the guy I'd been stringing along, that I was ready to commit and move forward with our relationship, so yeah, that was kind of a big deal. However, the psychic carried on about the winds of change, a shift in power and a variety of other things that I tuned out and left me wondering if I'd wasted my money since she couldn't give me anything more specific.

My money wasn't wasted on the tram ticket though as this was the first year it was open so early, thanks to a less than usual amount of snowfall this season.

Plus, it would be a great place to snap some photographs and hopefully secure a photographer's spotlight in the next issue of The Jamboree, a local touristy publication shipped to the major centres, promoting local attractions about my idyllic mountain town.

I checked my flight time against my phone, satisfied with a cushion of extra time, giving me a chance to double check my bag was well packed. Inside the trunk was a warmer winter jacket and a thick pair of mittens I used when skiing. Temperatures at the summit were reported to be about 12 degrees Celsius colder than what was at the main parking lot, which for an April day was still on the cool side. For good measure I added my scarf and hat to the backpack and slipped into my warmest winter boots. I tossed my thermos inside, securing it in place and checked on the battery meter of my good camera. Lots of life left – perfect since I'd planned on hiking up the trails and taking a whack of pictures. The view of the town nestled into the canyon of a few mountains was a sight to behold, and due for a proper update in brochures. I couldn't wait to snap the breathtaking scene.

Backpack slung across my shoulders, I locked my car and crossed the parking lot. Crowds of people were gathered on the platform and how lucky was it that I'd be joining them? I held my purse a little tighter as I went over to the waiting tram car, sauntering past small groups of tourists, all chatting excitedly.

A clock announced its time with an old-fashioned bell sound, clanging three times. I was catching the next flight at 3:10. Shielding my eyes against the rays of gorgeous sunlight, I followed the cable off the main docking station all the way up. I could see what was likely my ride slowly making its descent down the mountain. One going up, one going down, passing at the half-way point.

I sent a quick text to my boyfriend Noah, just to say hi and how I was looking forward to tonight. It was a huge step for me, committing to someone, but Noah was the cream of the crop. He was sweet and even tempered, and the fact that he worked as a ski instructor at Marmot Basin, a few kilometres away, didn't hurt either. He was strong and muscular, a body I was looking forward to surrendering myself to. Noah was good to me, and I was lucky to have him in my life.

The tram arrived and unloaded its smiling occupants, even if one mentioned how much warmer it was down here. I took that as my cue to make sure I was well bundled, as I didn't handle extreme cold too well. Slowly, after a few people boarded, I showed my flight ticket and stepped into the car where one of the ladies had bathed in her perfume and reeked up the tight confines.

I cracked the window open a touch, and when the tram guide looked at me with a questioning look, I tapped the camera I had the hindsight to dangle from my neck. The pictures were going to be amazing, if I didn't die from a lack of breathable air.

"Ready for takeoff," the operator, whose nametag read *Jaysen,* said into a walkie-talkie like radio while the folding doors slid closed and locked into place.

The car pitched forward for a heartbeat and suddenly, we were off, suspended above the parking lot, and climbing above the treetops. My stomach plunged into the depths of my boots before slowly traversing its way back up.

Pointing my camera around since I had the good fortune to be at the back of the tram, I snapped multiple pictures, including my car and the main platform station. The fresh breeze was refreshing, diluting the high concentration of floral to a nice fragrance of crisp mountain air mixed with the damp smell of melting snow. We travelled up into the sky, all the while Jaysen rambled on about the different mountain peaks visible (Mount Robson Canada's tallest mountain, was visible to the west on a clear day like today), when the tram originally opened (in 1964) and the extensive renovations completed over the past couple of years and why the huge grand opening next weekend was a big deal. He mentioned the restaurant was not yet operational but, should the need for hunger fill us, the gift shop was well stocked with packaged treats. Regardless, I brought my own, and kicked the bag at my feet to ensure it was still there.

Higher up the mountain side the tram pulled us skyward, and my breath held in my lungs. Over to the east there sat a low hanging cloud, shadowing a small part of the forest. It was magical – like something from a fantasy show – and I happily pointed the camera toward it and rapidly filled my memory card.

We docked seven minutes after leaving the main platform, and the tram car let out a sigh as the people exited. Most headed inside the building right away as the air was considerably colder and took your breath away. A breeze sliced at my face and lips with a stark reminder to reapply a fresh coat of lip balm for protection. Walking across the wooden sidewalk over to a bench, I pulled out my hat and scarf and wrapped myself up in them, after giving my lips a rub from the vanilla scented Chapstick. Once I was snuggled in, the temperature became bearable. Plus, the sun was shining, and that always helped to take the edge of the crispness away.

I walked along the boardwalk, beyond the building. The view was spectacular, majestic even. Snow-capped mountain tops peaked high above fluffy clouds, but the skies were a crystal-clear shade of azure. As I gazed down into the valley, the town of Jasper was visible and what had to be a mile-long train was currently snaking its way through. My camera clicked a nice rhythm as I tried to capture the beauty. The crisp air cleared my head, and I inhaled sharply through the warmth of my scarf so as not to freeze my lungs solid. There's nothing quite like mountain-fresh air to fill you with peacefulness and relax you to your core. Releasing that breath, I knew I'd picked the right place to come and think.

Beyond the edge of the boardwalk, there was still plenty of snow, although some had melted off and the tips of jagged rocks pierced through. Stepping off the wooden structure, the pebbles beneath my boots shifted with each step I took until I walked onto the frozen white tundra where it crunched instead. I turned and snapped a picture of the upper tram station, with mountain peaks in the background and the boardwalk in the foreground. An incoming tram car approached on the eastern side. It docked and the new crowd pushed free of the tight space, spilling out onto the boardwalk. I zoomed in to capture the wonder on their faces, and to watch them take that first cold gasp of air.

One face called out to me, and I zoomed in further, not believing the vision through my telephoto. A face I hadn't seen in years. A heartbreaker in the disguise of a Greek God. Truly. His dark hair, those olive-green eyes and skin so golden, it was nearly unnatural, except for him it was. Born in Greece, but raised in the same city as me, we went to the same high school where we met and fell in love, until our university careers took us in different directions and we couldn't make a long distance relationship work. Plus, at the end of things, he turned out to be a major jerk.

I turned off my camera with a sigh and turned my back to Alessandro. Just like the past ten years, I was going to avoid him. I had to. My heart was at stake and it had taken long enough to heal to the point where I could start to trust and open up to others. The area was large enough, and last I remembered, he wasn't into hiking up mountain trails. Neither was I really, but I was about to start.

Chapter
TWO

Alessandro Petrakis.

The name a whisper in the blowing winds as I pulled my camera close and shrunk into my scarf and pulled my hat lower. I stopped to stare at the sign a few yards away from the boardwalk, and if its words were true, it was a leisurely forty-five-minute hike to the peak with some rocky parts and a steep section. Probably meant for summer climbers on its worn-out path, but covered in snow like it was, I'd venture a guess it would be a much longer climb.

Whatever. As long as I was in back in the tram before its final departing five o'clock return, it was all good.

I focused on heading up, readjusting my backpack, and pulling my hat down a little lower. The ends of my hair smacked me in the face as I huffed and puffed up the slight incline. It made me feel as if I were in the worst shape of my life, which couldn't be further from the truth. The air this high up was much thinner than what I was acclimatized to and made breathing more difficult than I expected.

At a restable incline, I stopped and pointed my camera up the mountain. The snow made it difficult to see the path that had been so clearly marked on the sign, so I decided it was maybe in my best interests to not proceed much further. Without a tracking beacon or the like, no one would be able to locate me if I got lost, and without a clearly defined trail, I wasn't taking any chances. Besides, my cell phone had zero reception up this high. Aside from being able to take a few decent pictures, it was pretty useless. I could just outwait my former boyfriend until he exited onto the tram. Hopefully, it happened before the end of the day.

I stepped off to the side and swept a rock free of a light dusting of snow. Even through the edge of my winter jacket and my jeans, the cold seeped through to my butt, freezing it almost upon impact. After a few breaths, it became tolerable, allowing me once again to capture the beauty of nature.

Below me, bundled up crowds milled about the boardwalk and only a brave few stepped off and ventured about as far up the trail as I'd gone. Even as the wind howled, there was something serene about being here. The nearby mountain peaks were crystal clear and beyond that, I could see for miles.

Gazing down the dark green and rocky mountain slopes, to the valley far below, was my town, my home, looking as if I was searching it out on Google maps. I snapped a few more pictures, zooming in on the finer things I couldn't make out otherwise.

Twisting to my right, and facing into the whistling wind, through the zoom lens I spied an outcropping of rocks where someone made an Inukshuk, pointing toward the upper tram station. Beyond the sculpture was a pair of red chairs. The view from those must be even more spectacular, especially in the summer. Glacier Lakes, blue-green gems of mountain fed water, were in abundance and I inhaled deeply, pretending I could smell the freshness. Instead, my nostrils stuck together, ruining the perfect moment. It was much colder than I anticipated, and despite the layers I had on, I was starting to shiver.

A gust of wind blew up the side of the mountain, the strength of it nearly pushing me off the rock. I threw my eyes to the building below and the crowds of people on the boardwalk at once stopped moving, and in the next heartbeat pushed their way into the station.

Curious about what happened, I rose and snapped a few pictures of the station and descended down the dried-out snow, over a rough patch of pebbles and onto the boardwalk.

Earlier, when I'd stepped off the tram and onto the station's wrap-around walkway, there'd been a gentle vibration under my feet, likely from the engines working to cable the tram cars up and down the mountain. Now as I stood there motionless, there was no vibration. It was as still as I was cold. My heart picked up its speed as I raced toward the west door of the station.

People were crammed in everywhere and the murmur was louder than what I expected. A quick glance to my left and I'd accidently caught Alessandro's attention, who gazed at me with wide-eyed surprise. The one person I'd hoped to avoid. Turning away, I faced the older lady beside me, old enough to pass for my aunt.

"What's going on?" I asked. Maybe she had an idea, or maybe she heard something.

"The station lost power."

"Oh, okay." Likely wasn't too big a deal. These things happened in town all the time, and when they did the backup generators kicked in and all was fine. Until main power returned, it was business as usual. Visitors to the town never even knew when it happened.

I cocked my head and craned my neck to see where the tram cars were. One was parked in the west dock, which meant the other was down at the main station, since they traveled at opposites. When one car was at the top, there was one loading at the bottom. If it were a true emergency, they could probably fill the car to capacity and release it back down to the main station, right? It was all cables.

I was heating up from the inside wearing my thick winter clothes and being tightly packed into a small area with so many others wasn't helping, I needed to escape, and crowds weren't my thing either. Since the power loss wasn't an emergency situation, I pushed my way back out onto the boardwalk where it was easier to breathe, despite the cold, gusty winds, and thinner air. Making my way over to the edge and closer to the east side docked car, I glanced down the mountain and surveyed the cables connecting the upper and lower stations. The thick black wires undulated in the wind but other than that, there was no movement. The tram car beside me slammed into its dock from a powerful gust of air, and I jumped from the force as it shook the boardwalk.

A lady poked her head out the door and waved at me. "Hey, you, with the red hair. The manager or owner wants to talk to us all at once."

My heart fell off the edge of the mountain. That wasn't promising.

Swallowing, I made my way inside and glanced around. I connected once again with Alessandro, who with his pinched expression and a fading of colour, looked like a man trying to be brave. I remembered how he used to be in times of stress. He hadn't changed an ounce.

"Excuse me, ladies and gentlemen." A voice broadcast over the speaker system. "I'm Tony DeMarcas, the manager of the Upper Summit Platform. I'm here to tell you…" There was a short pause. "Due to the sudden wind gusts, we have lost power to this station. We've radioed down to the main station and they are aware of our predicament. There's nothing to worry about though, as they are working on restoring the main power. In the meantime, all descending flights are on hold."

Obviously. I rolled my eyes and glanced around the room as murmurs circulated. We were safe. It's not like we were stranded or anything, and once the power was restored, they'd pack the trams as full as could be and we'd be leaving. Once again, I scanned the room, counting quickly to give me a quick estimate. There were roughly a hundred people in the inside observation area, something in the ballpark of four cars full, if the operator had been correct on his twenty-five-person occupancy on the trams. That was nothing. At least we weren't stuck in the tram just waiting and dangling. That would be terrifying.

I was more worried about having a possible conversation Alessandro than I was about the situation. When power restored, all would be fine. Give them an hour to do whatever it was they needed to do.

In the meantime, I needed to escape from the watchful gaze from the man who once held my heart. I shook my head softly and turned away from view, slinking out the doors, back outside into the frozen tundra. There was lots of time for the power to come back on and take me down. My date with

Noah was in three hours. It would be tight, but doable. It afforded me plenty of time to take in the sights.

Heading over to the back of the building, I found a bench in full sunlight on the western side which also happened to be out of the windy gusts. Although it didn't present much of a view, aside from looking up toward the peak, it was warm enough I could remove my hat and loosen my scarf. From deep within my backpack, I removed the sealed thermos of hot chocolate and took a sip, the sweet minty chocolate taste swished around my mouth.

"Corrine, is that really you?"

Although it had been ten years, his voice was still mostly the same, perhaps a touch deeper. But hearing my name made my heartbeat faster. Not necessarily a good faster though. Not anymore.

I shut him out and nodded.

"Wow. You look great."

With that, my eyes popped open, and I took him in. "Really? I'm sitting down under a thick layer of winter clothing."

"Still." He stood there with his hands in his heavy wool pockets. "May I sit down?"

"Sure." I twisted the lid on the thermos tightly and pushed it back into my bag.

"Happy birthday."

I was floored he still remembered, considering throughout our time together, we'd only celebrated two of my birthdays; my seventeenth and my eighteenth. Too many moons ago.

"How've you been?"

"Still hurting." I stood, and yanking my bag off the bench, marched away.

Alessandro was not what I wanted to deal with right now, or ever. He'd closed the book on us before I even had the chance to figure out it was happening.

Leaving Ales to sit in stunned silence, I walked and read every sign mounted around the perimeter of the boardwalk, looking intensely enough at the mountain ranges I should've had them committed to memory. Instead, I had to read the damn things over and over again because I couldn't get the voice and sight of Alessandro out of my head.

As much as I tried to conjure up other images and have my mind control my body, my body fought equally as hard remembering all the good times we'd once shared. There were so many to choose from. The competition between mind and body raged on and in a dirty move, my mind flashed an image I'd swore I never wanted replayed. For now, the battle was over. Anger and hurt flooded my systems, and a low growl rolled out, freezing in the crisp air.

Why did he need to be up here? I was happy without having seen him over the years. Well, maybe not happy-happy, but I was trying. It's hard to get over a love like we had. In so many ways it had been perfect. We were made for each other. The key word being *made.*

Foot traffic on the boardwalk stopped and like a game of telephone, people relayed a message to me. "That manager guy needs us inside. Now."

Not concerned about a lack of power like the other tourists, I wasn't too bothered to race my way back inside and stand like sardines squished together.

Instead, I stood by the slightly opened western-facing door where I couldn't hear anything Tony said. "What's going on?" I leaned toward a guy who stood beside his wife and gripped the shoulders of his child.

He greeted me with a strong *shhh,* and I scanned the guests, involuntarily looking for the one person I really didn't want to see.

A crackling from the PA system silenced the murmuring crowds and directed my attention to the ceiling.

"Thank you. Once again, I'm Tony, the manager of the Upper Summit Platform. I've been in conversation with our lower platform to try and locate the source of our power failure. It seems that the power loss is only affecting the upper platform station as they have power on the main station."

Gasps rippled through the crowds.

"That being said, we are unable to send you back to the main station via the tram cars, since our backup generator doesn't have the power capabilities to operate at such high rates of power consumption."

"Can't we just load the cars and let them go to the bottom?" A gruff voice bellowed out a question.

"As simple as that sounds, no, we can't. Our carriages are hydraulically lifted and mechanically locked."

"Are you saying we're trapped up here?"

"Not at all. We've been connected with a helicopter company out of Hinton. They're flying two helicopters up to us and we'll evacuate everyone off the mountain that way."

The chatter ranged from excitement of riding in a helicopter to fear. At this point, I wasn't sure where I was on that scale.

"It'll take them a bit of time to arrive and while we wait, I'm going to ask for your names and size of your party. We're going to send our older guests and families first, in a relaxed and easy manner. Please don't worry, there's enough light and time to make sure everyone gets off the mountain tonight. As the rescue operations get underway, I'll need everyone to hang out in the observation area and to stay away from the back of the boardwalk and the trail systems. The helicopters need that space to land."

My heart beat a little quicker. I didn't like the sound of needing to be rescued per se but was pleased knowing they'd found a solution to getting us safely off the mountain and in a helicopter to boot. That had always been a dream of mine, however, it was beyond my budget. My psychic was right again – it was going to be an exciting weekend. I'd finally check a dream off my bucket list. I checked my watch. Time was ticking, but perhaps as a single guest, I'd be able to slip into one of the first flights.

Amazingly enough, the guests acted calmly and lined up in an organized fashion to add their names to the list, and what surprised me even more was how quickly I advanced to the front. To pass the time, I took a few more photos, mostly of the observation area, and the line of guests when I was still at the back.

Before I knew it, I was the next in line, and like the person ahead of me, said, "Corrine Wright, party of one." Quickly, I scanned the list as Jaysen, the tram operator, added my name in spot number eighty-five. For what I could make out quickly, most of the names were large groups, or at the very least, judging by the weird squiggly lines between names, a couple. Sigh. But I hadn't noticed Alessandro's name on the list, and he wasn't in the line behind me, so I inquired.

"No, he's not on here." He ran a finger over the scrawled names.

Good grief, what was wrong with me? I shouldn't be concerned about the guy who hadn't been called or explained his abrupt departure on us. "Please add him. Party of one, or if it helps, put him with me." Where the hell was he? Why was he not here? What was going on in his head?

It hit me like a Mack truck. The forthcoming rescue. Being stranded.

Ironically, Ales had a fear of being abandoned and my heart went out to him, knowing exactly how that felt. I shifted my bag and casually walked out the door, constantly searching for the guy who broke my heart to make sure he was okay.

Chapter
THREE

Surely, I was beyond messed up, I had to be. I wandered outside the east doors, searching for my former boyfriend. Finally, hidden behind a group of people, I spied him tucked into the spot we'd chatted at earlier, away from the wind but in the full light when he wasn't being people eclipsed.

"Hey," I said, advancing toward him. "Plan on staying up here permanently?"

He gazed up at me, the depths of his eyes holding fear. "No." But the word was as ghostly as his expression.

Compelled by a force I didn't understand, I sat beside him, remembering how bad his anxiety could be. "It's going to be okay."

"You don't know that. I don't know that. Even Tony the manager doesn't know that." His voice quivered more than the treetops with each passing gust.

I zipped my jacket higher. "They're bringing in helicopters to get us."

Even with his coat on, he started shaking, and as bundled as he was, I knew it wasn't because it was cold. If things hadn't changed much over the past ten years, there would be a way to counteract his building anxiety if he didn't bring his meds.

"Do you have your pills?"

"They're in my bag."

I checked under the bench and all around.

"In my car." His breath came in spurts.

Shit. Okay, no meds, no immediate way to calm him. Damn. People milled about and the volume of their conversations made it difficult to think clearly, but I needed a plan. I wasn't a monster; I couldn't just leave him like this. He needed to relax and take a couple of deep breaths and regain a smidge of control again. There was no reason for him to panic and worry. We were perfectly safe. Although, when someone is having an anxiety attack, it's hardly reassurance.

I hesitated. Would it work here? Inhaling a lungful of crisp mountain air, I stared into the depths of those olive-green eyes, marvelling at the unique shade. It was frightening to see the haunted panic jumping over his face, the twitch on the left side of his lips and the determined way he fought the rapid blinking I'd known him to have. I hesitated again. Could I do this?

"Give me your hand." My own mitten came off and I tucked it between my legs to keep it warm.

His gaze volleyed between my left and right eye before it fell to his hand. Slowly, he removed his glove.

I wrapped my hand around his and placed his palm on my leg, breathing deeply and trying to not enjoy the pool of heat spreading across my thigh. It was ridiculous this power he still had over my body. Relaxing my shoulders, I breathed deeply. Twice. "I want you to tell me five things you see." Unable to look him in the eyes, I explored the terrain myself.

"Mountain peaks." The twitch beside his lip doubled in its movement. "And a couple... selfie with the mountain... behind them..."

"Perfect, remember to keep breathing." I gave his hand a squeeze. "What else?"

"A rock... jutting out of the snow. A kid hitting its parent. A cat..." There was a hitch in his breath.

"What?" I searched in the direction he looked. It'd be beyond weird to see something as domesticated as a house pet at this elevation. In the distance, I spotted what Ales must've thought was a common pet, but it was far from being a cat. It was a hoary marmot, a rodent found in these parts. I didn't laugh at his error, nor bothered to correct him. He wasn't there yet. "What are four things you can hear, and remember, try to match your breathing to mine. I'll squeeze your hand with the inhale and relax with the exhale."

He shuddered beside me but started listing

things off while he closed his eyes and focused on the surroundings. Back in high school, he'd have the worst panic attacks, almost to the point he thought he was having a heart attack and dying, which just made the whole episode even scarier. Somehow, getting him to use his senses and bring him down always worked. I was counting on it now. The last thing the tram station needed was a medical emergency.

"Good job. Now, I need you to tell me three things you feel."

People milled about, paying us no attention. That was the best thing for Ales. One family walked by and the little boy clung to his dad, complaining in whimpers how scared he was.

Ales hitched his breath and I tossed off my other mitt, releasing my grip from his hand and firmly placing them on his face. Damn his cheeks were soft. Even the whiskers were nice. I clamped both my hands and stared into his eyes. "Ales, I need you to tell me three things you feel. Right now."

His voice elevated in pitch. "I… feel…"

From the corner of my eye I watched the family walk away. Thank God. That's all he needed now, especially combining with me asking him what he heard. For good measure, I shot daggers at the child's back.

He cleared his throat. "I feel… cold. The tip of my nose is very cold."

"Keep going." I tried to keep any urgency

out of my voice as I wanted him to reach a more calming state in the shortest amount of time possible.

"I feel your warm hands. It's nice."

I rolled my eyes. As sweet as the comment was, it wasn't going to change anything between us.

"I feel a breeze."

"Good. That's three. Now tell me two things you smell." This was always harder for him, and I figured it would be doubly harder on the summit platform where everyday scents were in short supply. However, the harder he focused, the less he'd worry about what his body was putting him through.

"I smell vanilla."

Vanilla? Oh right, before I put my mitts on, I rubbed on some slightly scented hand lotion. "That's because of me. What else can you smell?"

"Mint chocolate."

It took me a second to match that to its owner. "You can smell that?" A laugh was on the edge of my tongue. Apparently, I'd added a little too much peppermint to my hot chocolate for it to still be lingering in my mouth. At least it was a fresher smell.

In his cheeks, the muscles relaxed. He was coming down from the worry high, and in response to that, I let go of his face.

"Please, that was nice." His eyes opened and a pleading expression filled his face. "I've missed that."

Wait, what? With my hat pulled low over my ears, that must've been the reason for hearing his words the way I did. There's no way he could've missed my touch, if so, he would've tried to contact me at some point to apologise and make up. But no, he up and left and never turned back. However, one look at his face and I saw the truth there, bright as the sun.

His breath had calmed, and the wisps of warm air on exhale proved it. "I've missed you, Corrine."

Nausea settled in, and my limbs were as heavy as ever. A brief moment of falling through thin air wrapped around me and threatened to do me in. I shook my head and forced myself to stand, my legs so weak I needed to brace myself. How long had I waited to hear that? My brain sent signals to my foot to move and only after a few sharp breaths did they follow their command and slowly I retreated from the area, my words a weak whisper. "I can't. I'm sorry, Alessandro, but I just can't."

Chapter
FOUR

You'd have to be deaf to have missed the sound of the rotor blade noise as the helicopter climbed up the mountainside. Eager to see, the people pushed their way onto the boardwalk surrounding the platform. The helicopter flew beside the station, coming up on the eastern side. As it went to set itself down, dust and snow flew in all directions and I shielded my face with my arm.

The pilot remained in his seat, as another jumped out and pushed back the expectant crowds. Truly, it was a sight to watch the helicopter land on a mountain summit.

The crowds were encouraged back into the building and Tony spoke over the PA. Even inside the building the noise from the rotors was deafening.

"Ladies and Gentlemen, please." He was practically yelling, but the people were quiet. "I want the Millar family of five and the Singh couple of two to go to the east doors and the co-pilot will brief you quickly and take you over to the helicopter. The next family will be the Bessette, party of six, along with Josef Summerland. Please be ready when the next aircraft arrives in a few minutes. I'll post up a list on the east doors of who's following after that."

Knowing I wasn't on the first flight out, or even the second, was no big deal, so I waited while the mass of people pushed around to get a glimpse of their names on the list. After a few minutes of pacing around the observation area, staying clear of the west doors I'd been watching in case Alessandro breezed through, I inched my way over and scanned the list. My name was on the ninth spot. Yes! I'd still have some time to get ready for my date with Noah.

Speaking of which, I pulled out my phone and typed out a quick text.

Still up on Whistler's Mountain waiting for a flight down. Will touch base when I'm back on the main platform.

I hit send and watched, waiting for the 'delivered' message to appear. Nothing. At the top of my screen there was a no signal sign, which of course there wouldn't be. I was on top of a mountain.

To preserve what was turning out to be an interesting visit, the dealing with Ales aside, I stepped outside onto the west side of the station, ignoring my former boyfriend, and walked to the back of the building. I snapped a few pictures that would make a neat conversation piece in my photobook. How often does a helicopter land up on the mountain to rescue people? Since I've lived in town, none that I was aware of. Maybe a couple of times near the ski hill, but that was to catch skiers caught in an avalanche. For the most part, this area was fairly calm for mountain rescues.

Under the guise of readjusting the shutter speeds and f-stops, I peered at Ales sitting on the bench. He wasn't shaking anymore, so hopefully the anxiety had passed with the arrival of the helicopters. It was rude of me to have left him so abruptly, but it was impossibly hard to be around that guy. My mind would never forgive him, and yet my body would instantly submit to his sexiness and the kindness he once had. No matter what happened between us, my body strongly remembered the good times, and it wanted more. Even now. I'd just have to keep the images of the hard times in the forefront to remind myself how long it took for those wounds to heal, and how some of them hadn't fully recovered.

I looked away for just a moment, and when I returned to his spot, he was gone.

"Hey." His voice whispered from behind me.

I checked out the space between the bench and me, curious how he managed to walk that distance without me seeing. It was a total mystery.

"Hey." Aiming my camera with the new settings, I clicked away on the family boarding the helicopter.

"Thank you…" His inhale was sharp, he must still be struggling. Poor guy. "For before, for grounding me."

"Of course, I wasn't going to let you suffer." He may have damaged me, but in his time of need, I had to rise above and be better than that. "Are you feeling better?"

"I will be when I get off this mountain."

I shrugged and a gust of wind flapped the end of my scarf in my face.

Alessandro pulled and tied it away. "Where are you on the list? Did you check?"

"Ninth. So still a bit." I zoomed the frame out, trying to include all of the helicopter and a mountain peak in frame.

His head bobbed. "And me?"

He knew me too well, and I hung my head, swallowing the lump forming. "You're the third last flight." Likely his anxiety will hit new levels before that moment comes, and if I'm not up here he'd be on God's good humour to keep him calm. "Can you trade with anyone?"

"As if. They all want to get down off the mountain too."

Yep, that I understood. I'd trade my ticket with his, but Noah waited for me and without a way to communicate with him, it was best that I held on to my spot. I clicked away again.

"Are you a photographer?"

I sighed and rested the heavy camera against my chest, the strap tugging on my neck. "Not really, but I work for a tour company in town, and hope that maybe some of my pictures could be hung up in the shop."

"Ah, so you're a tour operator?"

I shook my head. No, what I did was a long way off from what I'd studied to become back in my university days.

"What do you do then? Are you still in engineering?"

Don't I wish? Oh, how the dream can change so much when you lose all hope. I wasn't embarrassed by my job, not at all. It paid the bills and allowed me to live my life. Yeah, I wasn't making the same kind of cash an engineering career would've brought me, but I was reasonably happy.

"What are you up to these days?" Alessandro loved talking about himself, and no doubt, time hadn't changed that over the years.

"I'm working out of Victoria as a whale watching tour guide." His eyes searched mine.

Tour guide? That was a huge leap from his marine biology aspirations, and I stifled a giggle.

"You think I'm a sell out, don't you?"

Damn my lack of ability to stop my feelings from spreading across my face. "Not at all." I swallowed and twisted away, refocusing on the helicopter as the noise from it changed swiftly.

"Because I'm not. It's very exciting work.

I'm the marine biologist on board and we track the pods in the bay. I love my job."

Not quite the direction he left me for, but I took back my original thought. At least it's still in his field. Ever since I'd known Ales, that was what he wanted to do. He was a natural swimmer and felt most at peace in the water, no doubt the company was a natural fit for him.

"That's great. I'm happy for you." I tried my best to be sincere.

A higher pitched noise rolled off the mountainside, and the helicopter lifted up and flew over around to our side. Not thinking in time, I lifted my camera just as the chopper descended over the ledge.

Ales leaned against the wooden rail and tipped his head back up to the sun and following suit I copied him. I had to admit, the sunshine felt nice. Seemed we had so little of it lately.

People walked by, back into the observation area, leaving us alone for the most part. Quietness swarmed around me, and the blowing breeze whistled off the building. Ales tucked himself further into his coat.

Words escaped me, not that it mattered because I didn't know what to say or how to say it without it being laced with venom. There was so much I wanted to say, or scream at him, but this wasn't the place. Another day, another time. Maybe.

But I wasn't the only one silent. Ales

looked thoughtful and introspective as he stared up at the sun with his eyes closed. The dimple between his eyebrows grew deeper as the clock advanced. Unable to stare into his handsome face any longer, I tore my gaze away.

Another helicopter advanced up the eastern side of the platform and set down in the snow beyond the edges of the platform. Once again, they loaded it up with four adults and two little kids, who through the lens of the camera looked absolutely terrified. Ready with the camera on standby, as the chopper lifted off and headed west, I clicked to my heart's content. There was some great footage, at least I hoped. It would make a neat book but I doubted I'd be able to make any money off these, there were too many people snapping pics with their cell phone cameras and they were going to be on the platform before I was able to. That meant they'd load them to their social media accounts and get the retweets and likes, and by time I got down there, it would be old news.

Typical.

Chapter
FIVE

For two and a half hours, I watched one helicopter at a time arrive, load up and descend down the mountainside. Guests lined up in an orderly fashion, awaiting instructions to head out onto the boardwalk and over to their ride down.

The wind gusts were causing some problems and one chopper, upon landing, blew sideways to the west before it was able to set down. Only two more loads and I'll be on my way.

Since the helicopter incident with load five, the manager wanted us all to stay indoors for our own safety. Besides, it was much warmer inside with all the body heat, and as I nabbed a lone seat by the window, was also a great place to watch and photograph the chopper rise up to our level.

Digging out a pack of peanuts, courtesy of the overpriced gift store, I poured a handful into my palm and dumped them into my mouth.

Alessandro pointed to the vacated seat

across from me. "May I?"

It's not like there were a variety of other options for him, so I begrudgingly agreed.

"It's getting windier."

I couldn't disagree. The treetops appeared to flatten with every wind gust, and the tram car docked outside slammed into its base, rattling the windows. It was slightly unnerving.

"And the sun's dipping behind the peak of the range."

Knowing exactly where he was going with this, but as not to give him a further reason to panic, I shrugged off his comment. The sun was a good hour from actually dipping beneath the horizon, but once it sunk behind the peaks, visibility reduced dramatically.

He looked around as he spoke and leaned in close. "The wind alone is enough to delay our rescue, but the darkness will definitely kibosh it."

My eyes narrowed. "What are you saying?"

"I'm saying, some of us aren't leaving here today." He pointed toward his own chest.

"You're crazy." I twisted off the cap to my thermos and took a sip.

"Maybe. But I'm right. They're just not telling us this good piece of news." The sarcasm was deep as it rolled off his tongue, but I followed his gaze over to the manager, who was on the phone. His back was to the open area and his head was bent down.

"And, maybe, they're close to having the

power restored and we'll all be able to take the tram back down?" It was a guess at best. There had been no rumblings associated with a restoration of power, and as much as I didn't want to believe Alessandro was right, there was the distinct possibility of him being correct. But I hoped it waited a little bit before coming true. My flight down was two away.

As I stared at the back of the manager's head, the roar of rotor blades announced its appearance and the next group of seven headed out the doors.

After this flight, I was going home and eagerly, I pushed my thermos back into my bag in preparation.

"Can I ask the hugest favour from you?"

I stood and pulled my jacket up over my arms and shoulders. "I've already been more than courteous in having these conversations, Ales. I don't owe you anything." *You gave me that right when you refused to return my calls in my darkest hour and come help me.*

"You're right, you owe me absolutely nothing." He stood beside me, leaning in closer. "But you're the only one up here I know."

I scanned the room. It had to be true, the whole time he was up here, I hadn't seen him chatting with anyone else. "Your point?"

"Can you trade your ticket with someone on my flight?"

"Why on Earth would I do that?"

His brow wrinkled and he gave his neck a solid rub. Deep in his eyes, terror settled in for a long nap.

My words needed to be reassuring. "You'll only be a few rides behind me, and you'll be back at the main station a couple of hours from now." Deep down, based on how that last flight took off his could be, and likely would be, longer.

He shook his head. "I know you think I'm crazy, but some of us won't be going down. Not tonight."

"Yeah, you're crazy." It wasn't the first time I thought that either, and I wasn't going to allow myself to be trapped up here with him, in the event his intuition turned out to be correct.

"If you're so confident we'll all be evacuated before we're plunged into darkness, would you consider staying and flying down with me?"

They had two helicopters in operation; as one descended, the other was ascending, just like the trams had. There weren't a lot of people remaining either. "But I..."

His face crumpled, and he jammed his hands into the pockets of his wool coat.

"I can't. I have plans for tonight."

"Oh yeah?"

It was said with such disbelief, like how in the world could I be with someone else? Yes, it had taken years and a change of scenery moving to a new town to overcome that crippling fear and loss, but why did he say it like it was big news? I squared my shoulders. "Why do you sound so surprised? You may have held my heart for the longest time, Alessandro Petrakis, but I'm no longer yours."

Tentatively, he reached out to touch my arm and a too-quick smile crossed his face. "And no doubt, whoever he is, he's a lucky man."

"He's the best." And he'd been waiting for me long enough.

"So that's a no? You won't put your plans on hold to hang out with me?"

"Revenge is a dish best served cold." With that, I walked away. It was beneath me to be so cold and cruel, but I couldn't be around him. He still had a positive effect on me, and damn it, this time logic would win out over my heart. It had too.

I stood in line with my six other travelling mates. A few more minutes to go. I kicked at an imaginary rock and scuffed my boot across the floor. Whatever it took to not look in Ales' direction.

He wasn't evil, even if that's what my head wanted to remember. There had been so many good times. So many. Because we'd been in love, the purest form, and for a while we were the best versions of ourselves. He'd made high school better, and even when he took off to UBC, he still managed to come home and make me his number one. The final time aside, he'd been an upstanding guy, the one who held the key to my heart. The one I swore I had a future with.

And Noah?

I was sure the tram losing power was gossip fodder in town. There wasn't much else to do, and gossip travelled through like wildfire. Even working at the ski hill, he had to have heard something. He'd understand if I were a little late, especially if he tried to text me and my texts were undeliverable.

Without really wanting to, my eyes fell to the list taped by the west doors. There was my name on the next flight, inside the red circle with my travel mates. Ales was down near the bottom, just four flights behind.

I sighed. His anxiety was already bad, and the clingy in him was starting to come out. Even a couple of hours fighting against that feeling was rough, and if I was the one who'd be able to make it bearable, I'd be an idiot to not help him out. Then again, we're talking four more flights and he'd be on his way. An hour tops, maybe two.

Damn it. Why did he put me in this position?

I read the list again, looking for a single name that didn't seem attached to anyone in the grouping of people. Taking a steely breath, I waivered on what I was about to do. Did I put Noah first, or Ales?

The rotor noise announced its incoming arrival.

I needed more time to weigh the decision. Oh, damn it anyway. "Deserie Williams?" I belted out in my loudest voice, cupping my hands around my mouth like a megaphone.

She appeared by my side instantly. "Yeah?" There was more than hope across her features.

"Would you like to swap places with me, and go now, and I'll take your spot?"

"For real?"

I nodded, feeling a tiny tug in my stomach. "Yeah."

"Hell ya. Thanks." She stood in my spot.

I pulled a pen out of my bag and drew an arrow between our names. It was done. I was now going down on a later flight. With Alessandro. Now to find him and tell him the news.

Chapter
SIX

Ales was hanging out in the furthest spot from the door but the closest to the window, the one with the full view of the western side and valley.

"Hey," I breathed out. Unsure if he would've heard me call out Deserie's name over the noise from the helicopter, I lightly tapped his shoulder.

He turned around slowly, the smile on his face spreading much faster. I'd always adored his sweet expression, the way his eyes lit up when he'd see me. Time hadn't changed that. "You stayed."

"I did." A huff bellowed out of me as I pinched the bridge of my nose to ward off the start of a stress headache. "I'm riding down with you."

"You have no idea what this means to me." He rose as I came closer to the table. "Have a seat."

"I intend on it." I shucked out of my jacket, draped it over the back of the chair and dumped my backpack on the seat beside me. "Thirsty?" I retrieved my thermos from my bag and twisted off the lid, tipping it in his direction.

He shook his head. "I grabbed an overpriced bottle of tap water from the gift shop."

"Suit yourself." I took a sip of the hot chocolate and put the lid back into place. "It's been quite the day." Why was I suddenly reduced to small talk? The stupidity of it made me laugh.

"What's funny?"

"I don't know. You and me? This situation? I'm not sure."

The noise in the room grew as the door opened, and my flight group headed out to the back of the boardwalk. It was hard to not feel a tad jealous. In ten minutes, maybe fifteen, I'd be walking over to my car as I dialled Noah's number. It was a painful enough thought to make me cringe. A couple hours more and then it would be my turn.

"So, we have time to kill. Tell me what you've been up to with your life."

"Yeah, we're not there." And I didn't feel sorry for stating that. Right now, my job here was to keep him grounded and to prevent him, as much as I could, from having an anxiety attack. "I'm not sharing anything personal with you, Ales. Not about my job, or my life or my recreational activities."

He put his hands up in a stop motion. "Fair enough. Nothing personal." He glanced at my backpack. "Do you still carry a deck of cards?"

"I used to but not anymore." That had been one of the ways we killed time, playing cards. Didn't matter what the game was – Canasta, Old Maid, Rummy – it was fun. Because it was with him. After things went south between us, I tossed the worn-out deck from its spot in one of the side pockets.

"Give me a minute. I'll be right back." Ales walked over to the mediocre gift shop and returned a minute later with a brand-new deck of cards, printed with a working tram station. With the flick of his nail, he punctured the plastic and unwrapped the cards.

"They accept credit cards?"

"Yes, I asked. Their machine uses the phone line."

No power yet. Damn. "I wonder if they'd let me use the phone?" It was spoken out loud although I'd wanted it to be an inside thought.

He shrugged out of his coat and folded it, setting it on the space beside him. "Maybe?"

"I really need to make a call. Be right back." Without a word, I headed over to the gift shop cashier, who was as old as a high school graduate, if that, but she had an old school name – *Gwen.* "Your phone line's working?" I looked at the phone on the desk beside her, just in case I was any way unclear about what I was asking.

"It is." Gwen narrowed her eyes suspiciously.

"Can I use it to make a quick call?"

Glancing around, she shrugged. "Sure." She flipped around the old school rotary phone, most likely the original one from when the station opened. Not surprisingly, she didn't move to give me any privacy.

Oh well. I lifted the receiver, checked for a dial tone, and put my finger into the first of nine numbers, watching as the dial rotated back to the starting position before dialling the second number. No wonder these things went out of style. It took forever to dial all the digits. Finally, it connected and a phone on the other end of the line rang but went straight to voice mail.

Figures.

"Hey, Noah. I'm going to be late for dinner. I'm stuck at the top of Whistler as the power went out, and there's no cell reception up here. Just waiting for my helicopter to come and rescue me. I'll touch base when I'm at the main station. Talk to you then." I hung up and flipped the phone around. "Thanks."

"Yeah, no problem." She resumed her seat on a stool and crossed her legs.

Oh, my sweet Noah. Had he heard about the power loss? There was no way to know. If his day was going as it normally did, he'd be hanging up his skis and having a hot shower. He was most definitely the hottest ski instructor on the hill, and I would know as that's how I met him. Lived in Jasper for years before I swallowed my fear and tried out skiing. Ran two people over with a loss of control, and he caught me, quite literally, before I took out a third, and suggested I join him for his next ski lesson.

I sighed. Tonight, we were going to make our relationship official, and, as a birthday gift to me, take things to the next level. I even had some new lingerie to show him and had planned to change into it when I got home. Which was going to be much later thanks to Ales' plea.

I shook my head and walked back to where Ales had dealt out the cards.

"Everything okay?" He cocked an eyebrow.

"Went to voicemail. But at least I got a message out." I sat and picked up my hand. "What are we playing?"

"Rummy."

"Really?" A great card game… for me. Ales had never learned to win or had always let me win. Regardless, victory had always been mine. I was a bit rusty since the last time I played was with him and his parents, but I wasn't as bad as I thought.

Without conversation, aside from the occasional *your turn* we played a few more hands, watching the next group line up and file out. I had to admit, it was all very civilized and under control. No one was losing their minds or freaking out. Thinking of the general anxiety Ales had, I stared at him, watching the tics on his face. All was good, for now.

The roar of an incoming helicopter filled the room again and the next grouping of people gathered near the east doors. Before I had time to sort my cards into proper suits and numerical order, they were out. Two rounds of back and forth, searching for either a heart to complete my set or a Queen to make my set of three a set of four. I just picked up the right card and called out rummy as the helicopter flew by the west windows and dropped into the valley.

Judging by the remaining few people still hanging out in the area, there weren't too many flights left. Just needed to pass this time and we'd be on our way.

Ales shuffled and dealt, his hands moving effortlessly as he rotated the cards and made a bridge before they all fell back together. Through his sweater-covered arms, it was easy to see the definition in his forearms, the way they used to wrap around me and hold me to him.

I blinked myself out of my thoughts and stared at the pile of cards begging to be picked up.

As much as I tried keeping my gaze laser focused to my starting hand, it was damn near impossible to not check out Ales – the thick dark hair he'd periodically ran his hands through while deep in thought and the way the wrinkle between his brows deepened as he contemplated his next move like it was rocket science and not just a card game.

He'd always been super serious about

gaming. Whereas I enjoyed the playing aspect more, he was a total gamer. It was fun watching his expression as I picked up the top card and saw how it would work. Tapping it against the table, I let the indecision of adding it and claiming another win or dropping it into the discard pile rise. A couple of deep breaths, as if it was some monumental choice. His eyes danced to the pile as I dropped my card. I didn't need it now. There'd be others.

Those beautiful dark eyes of his lit up and he grabbed the card, shoving into the space between his third and fourth card. "Hah-hah." He splayed his cards across the table. "Rummy."

It was a sweet victory.

I laid mine down. "Five."

"Damn it. Thought I caught you with a mittful."

"You should know I'm a better card player than that." That old Kenny Rogers song played in my head – *You have to know when to hold them, know when to fold them and know when to walk away.* I scooped up and tossed my cards onto the pile, waiting for Ales to add his. When he did, his hand lingered above the pile a little longer than necessary until I swept it away as I gathered the deck.

"Do you hear that?" He cocked his head to angle it towards the darkening windows.

"What?" I heard nothing at all.

"Just listen." His hearing had never been the best, but clearly something caught his attention.

I stretched out my neck, straining to hear whatever it was he heard. "I don't hear anything."

"Exactly."

"What do you mean *exactly*?" I rose at the same time he did, and a deep panic filled my soul, but I kept my roaring thoughts to myself, hoping I was wrong.

"Within ten minutes of a chopper leaving, the other one can be heard." Alex was talking more out loud to himself than he was talking to me. He tapped his watch. "The last one left almost fifteen minutes ago."

Yep, he was on the same train of thought I was, and my heart skipped a beat at the idea.

"The other hasn't yet made an appearance."

There was no need to strike a match and stoke the fire.

A loud voice beckoned our attention. "Ladies and Gentlemen, can I have your attention please?"

Oh shit. I looked over at Ales and watched the colour seep out of his face. He held onto the table with both hands and sat with a thump into the chair. We both knew what was coming.

Chapter
SEVEN

There were fifteen of us left in the room; twelve guests sitting around the tables, two staff members in their standard issue Tram uniforms leaning against the gift shop desk, and one manager, standing on a chair.

"Ladies and Gentlemen. It is with a heavy heart that I need to stand here and speak to you. I was hoping that the last three flights down would've been completed by now, but it seems the wind gusts and the settling darkness will delay our rides."

"By how long?" A voice to my right called out. He was an older man, middle aged, but the expression on his face spoke more volumes than the clipped tone his voice had.

The manager gulped. Even from a few feet away where I stood it was noticeable. It had bad news written all over it. "Until tomorrow."

"Tomorrow?" A woman gasped and the

chair she fell back into scraped across the floor. "Tomorrow? But…"

I looked over to Ales. He hadn't fared any better with the announcement. I walked around to his side of the table and reached for his hand. Damn, it was so soft, cold but soft. My fingers tingled just entwining my own between his. "It'll be okay."

"Why can't they rescue us in the dark?" The older man barked.

The manager straightened himself out. "The gusts make it difficult to land when they have full light, even with these experienced pilots. However, given the relatively tight landing area and the lack of sunlight, landing is damn near impossible in the dark."

"Damn near… so you're saying that there's a remote chance?" The guy rallied the small group of us using his hands and signalling we all rise. "So why don't we make that chance? We can all be out there on the boardwalk–"

"It's not the safer of the choices. They were lifting off from the parking lot below and an unexpected wind shear damn near blew them into the tree line. It's just not safe for them anymore."

"If the wind dies down?"

That had been a question I'd been ready to voice.

"Not tonight, unfortunately." His shoulders rolled in under the weight of his words. "There's no light back behind the station. The sun has set, twilight surrounds us. Like it or not, we're here for the night."

"For the night." Ales whispered the last three words and gripped my hand painfully.

I hung my head and blinked a few times to clear my field of view. Spending the night hadn't been in the plans. I was supposed to be home already, and if I hadn't given up my spot, I would be. Instead, I was now trapped on the top of a mountain with my ex-boyfriend and thirteen strangers. Perfect. Just perfect. I gritted my teeth as my heart pounded violently against my rib cage.

"So, what are we supposed to do?"

"What's your name, sir?" The manager asked.

"Gerald."

"Thank you, Gerald. For now, I am going to hunt for some blankets and flashlights, and I'll distribute those upon location. The gift shop will remain open for a while. We're in the process of turning off non-essential power pulls in order to keep the generator running for as long as possible. It's supplying us a bit of light…"

I looked up to the ceiling, just noticing that indeed there was a little bit of light. It was every third pot light, but it had still created enough luminescence to see.

"And a bit of heat. The outside temperature will drop considerably over night, but it'll be warmer in here than outside, so you'll all be safe. If you need the washrooms…"

He carried on about resorting to using the flashlights when needed, but to keep the use to a minimum so that they'd get us through the night.

Through the night.

The thought settled like a lead weight in the pit of my stomach. Ordinarily, a night was no big deal. A night trapped in my house was beyond manageable, even a night trapped at work. I had plenty of food, and power packs to operate my phone. Plus, I also had a thick pile of blankets on my bed to keep me warm. But this, this was all together different.

Ales squeezed my hand again.

"Sit." When he didn't move, I tugged him down. I grabbed his cheeks with my hands and stared into the depths of his darkening green eyes. The twitch under my hand was strong, and his blinks increased in speed. Not again. Not now. "We're going to be okay. I promise. Tony promises." And Tony better not have lied to us. "Everything we need, it's available to us. We're only stranded. We're not in dire needs. It's not like we crashed on the mountain, and we're struggling to stay alive. I swear, we'll be fine." I believed it in my heart and hoped that it was there in my voice and tone, as I was trying to convince myself as well. "Okay?"

A twitch increased on the edge of his lips.

"Repeat it back to me, Ales."

His head bobbed in tiny, jerk-like movements. "We're going to be okay."

"Say it again." *And say it so I'll believe it.*

"We'll be okay."

Damn. It wasn't enough to convince me, but for Ales' sake, I smiled. "That's it."

The pinched brow relaxed, and his tic slowed its pace. For now, it'd have to do.

"Keep breathing." I tapped out a slow and steady rhythm on his chest. His heartbeat pounded against my palm.

"If anyone needs to make a phone call, please come up and use the phone," Tony announced to the observation area.

Ales' breathing slowed, along with his blinks.

I waited a minute more until the twitch on the left side of his lips also relaxed its pace. "Do you need to call anyone? Your girlfriend, your wife?" Just because he wasn't wearing a ring, didn't mean anything. There were two guys at the shop who wives I'd met, and yet they never wore their rings. However, why hadn't I inquired about that before or while we played cards? Not that I cared one way or another. He wasn't mine. Hadn't been since he left me.

"I think I should."

At that comment, my heart did a quick plunge into my gut, which was completely ridiculous. I had Noah, and obviously, Ales had someone too. "Come on." I rose and pulled him up beside me. "I'll tag along and listen to the sweet nothings you'll whisper into her ear."

It was the wrong thing to say, but whatever. Try as I may to be strong and confident that the whole situation really was no big deal, inside, I was dying a little. I was spending my birthday with my ex-boyfriend and thirteen other strangers at the top of a mountain. My big plans went up in smoke, and like it or not, I had to call Noah and tell him I wasn't coming down until the light of day tomorrow. At least a good fourteen hours from now, assuming the first helicopter arrived with the sunrise, which was roughly around eight in the morning.

We waited in line, which was only two people deep. While Ales tapped his foot nervously, I scanned the gift shop, selecting with my eyes the items I was going to buy to sustain us through the night. There wasn't anything healthy aside from bags of peanuts, so it looked like it was going to be a high caloric intake kind of night with heavy fat-containing snacks and sugar-filled soft drinks. I'd need to hike up the mountain twice at least to burn it all off. Oh well, how often do you get to spend the night up on a mountain? I should've been recording this.

"Shit. I need my camera." I left Ales alone for less than a minute while I ran to my bag and pulled out my Canon. Before I headed back, I snapped random pictures of the phone line, which extended three people out from Ales, and pictures of the people hanging out at the tables, worry lines creasing their forehead. One zoomed in photo of a lady older than me, revealed tears in her eyes, and I found it deeply personal and touching enough I almost deleted the picture. For now, I'd keep it, and when I went through the pics on my computer, I'd blur her features, so she wasn't recognizable.

I made my way back to Ales and snapped a picture to the sign on the door. It would have everyone's names on it, so if and when I made the book, I could always look those people up. Maybe. Turning my camera towards the darkened windows, the remaining guests reflected in the orange hue from the pot lights gave a borderline romantic look to the place, although romance was the furthest thing from anyone's mind based on the tight expressions everyone wore.

It was going to be a long night. Happy birthday to me.

As Ales' turn came, he stepped over to the desk and dialed a number. It wasn't local. "Hey, Luce, it's me," he said in a voice that would've given me chills to have heard it across a telephone line. The deep baritone sadness was heartbreaking. "Listen, I'm going to be late as I'm stuck up on some mountain just outside of Jasper." He twisted away from me. "Yeah, I know. It was supposed to be a quick sightseeing trip on my way through, but it didn't work out that way... I can't talk long as there are a few people waiting for the phone... No, cells aren't working. Altitude problem... Yes, I should be there for the wedding... We're being rescued tomorrow... Thanks... And no, don't tell mom. She'd worry… Just make something up… I gotta go. Bye."

Ales hung up and gave me a once over, avoiding all contact. "I'll wait for you at the table."

I nodded and watched him walk away. Had he been referring to his own wedding? Quickly, I lifted the handset and painstakingly dialled. No surprise, it went straight to voice mail. I would've thought Noah would've been waiting by the phone for me to call. I left a brief message, explaining the overnight situation and told him I'd call in the morning. Short, simple, deeply painful.

Phone call completed, I breezed through the tiny gift shop, grabbing a few items I thought we'd need. A couple of bags of peanuts, along with a whack of junk food, and a couple of bottles of coke. The cashier rang everything up, but we waited for the next call to be completed before she could dial out on the credit card machine.

Purchases in hand, I set them down between Ales and I. "Everything okay?"

"Yeah."

"I couldn't help but overhear, the wedding you were referring to… Yours?" I divided everything and pushed half to his side of the table.

"Is that jealousy I hear in your voice?"

A huff blew out of me. "Not anymore." I twisted my chair and angled it away from the table. It wasn't jealousy, just insane curiosity. And why shouldn't he be married? He was a good-looking guy and was incredibly smart. Had a good job and a steady income. No doubt there was someone waiting for him back home.

Ales leaned on his forearms, the lip twitch gone and the blinking back to a normal rate. "No, it's not my wedding. Stavros is getting married on Sunday."

"Sunday? That's weird."

"You remember Stav, right? Never did anything the traditional way."

Which was true. Stavros was Alessandro's older brother, and always beat his drum to a different beat. Instead of taking four years to complete his architecture degree, he did it in two, graduating from university the same year Ales and I graduated from high school. "Tell me about him."

"What's to tell? He set up his own firm, fresh out of school, and now it's one of the most sought-after firms. He's exceptionally well off and had a kid last year."

"He has kids? Where would he find the time?"

"He's a fantastic father. All kids should be so lucky." There was a warm smile of affection on his face. "And finally, he decided to ask Lucy for her hand. Like Stav always does, he does things when he's good and ready."

"So, where's he getting married?"

"A church."

"And they have availability on a Sunday?"

"Apparently. It's the five-year anniversary date of when they met, so it was the date that mattered, not the day of the week."

I shrugged. "Cool." Dates were a big deal to the Petrakis Family. If anything new or important happened, it became a day of celebration. Ales remembered the first month anniversary of our first date, and insisted we celebrate it on the first year too. There was the first-year anniversary of the date we had sex for the very first time, the day we got our university acceptance letters, the day I broke my arm skateboarding. He remembered it all, and I'd always wondered if he had some giant notebook to write it all down in.

A relaxed expression hung on his face, and it settled me to see it. I was glad he was starting to calm down. "Tell me about your niece or nephew."

"Ah, sweet little Pierce. He's a robust little butterball with lungs you can hear from a mile away. And a smile to melt your heart and forget he can be so loud." He pulled his phone out and thumbed through an app, flashing it toward me.

"Aw, he's cute. Looks like your brother."

He turned the phone back and stared at it. "I guess. It's the eyes."

A family trait for sure and too many times I wondered about our own kids and if they would have his eyes or be stuck with my boring brown ones. The Petrakis eyes were dark and mysterious, yet warm and welcoming. It's what pulled me in the first time I met Ales way back in chem class.

"What about your family?"

"What? Oh yeah." For a moment, I'd

allowed myself to visit a happier time in my life – high school. A time when we were young and free, and recklessly in love. I filled my lungs with air and a bit of courage to open up. "Mom and Dad moved back to the East Coast, where they're living out their retirement years."

"East coast where?"

"PEI. They went on a vacation there years ago, and Mom said that was where they were going to live. So, when Dad retired last year, they went." She'd been so strong in her desire to go that Dad didn't bat and eye and happily obliged. As long as she was happy, he was happy. I envied that about their relationship.

"Wow, good for them. Pretty young to retire."

I nodded, keeping the jealousy monster at bay. "Julie married a stockbroker, and my parents took Jesse's advice and did very well on their portfolio. With that, they were able to retire a year ago and are now living the island life."

"Julie's married?"

My baby sister who had a man-sized crush on my boyfriend. "Yeah and get this." I twisted my chair around and leaned in closer. Not that anyone in the vicinity knew me or my family, but still. I was gossiping, not one of my finer traits. "On the eve of her high school graduation, which was what, six years ago?" I had to wrack my brain as she was five years younger than me, so trying to line up dates should've been easy, but for some reason I always struggled. "Anyways, she starts dating this Jesse. He's a nice enough guy, but he's five years older than me, so there's a big age gap between them. Anyways, he's quite successful and wines and dines Jules. By the end of that summer, they're engaged. And had this huge destination wedding in January."

"Seriously? Six months after going out?"

"Right?" I was on a roll now and laughed at how easy it had been to share that with him. "Yep. And a year after that, she had a son names Marcus. Sixteen months later, another son they named Adam and then a year ago, had a daughter they called Delilah."

"Jesus – three kids?"

"And all before the age of twenty-three." At that age, I was still trying to find myself and figure out what I wanted from life. When I reflected on me being twenty-three, it was depressing images of greys and long days wearing pajamas and not living my best life. Mind you, that really hadn't changed in the years following. There were minor moments of happiness, but the dreary was consuming.

"That's wild."

"That's a word for it. But she's living the executive life in Toronto. They have a nanny, a cottage out by the lake and a penthouse in New York City."

"Uber successful then?"

"Totally." Sucks that my niece and

nephews are so far away, I never see them except at Christmas, when they fly me out. Easy for them to do, since it's just lonely ole me with no spouse or kids.

Seeing their picture-perfect postcard sized family photo caused a raw, achy feeling to wash over me. It could've been me. It could've been us. Instead, it majorly sucked to be pushing thirty and have nothing to show for my life. No successful job, at least nothing I'd want to make a career out of. No spouse, and definitely no kids. To outsiders looking in, or even my family, I was a walking disappointment. That's why I moved to Jasper a few years ago. To escape the constant scrutiny. Although, not long after I moved, they all scattered to the wind as well.

"And what about you, Corrine? What have you been up to?"

"Living the dream, just not the one..." Ah, there was no point in being morose. Life handed me lemons, and I was still figuring out how to make lemonade out of them. I dismissed my spoken thought with a wave and turned to stare at the window, the achiness threatening to wash over me and drown me again.

"About that... About our dream." He twisted his hands together.

I shook my head and narrowed my eyes. "Not now. Not ever. We're stuck together until daylight. I'd rather not spend the night hating you."

"You hated me?"

A painful sigh bellowed in my chest, reminding me of the never healed scar on my heart. My words fell out in a low trembling voice. "That was wrong. I don't hate you. I hated what happened, and how you left me. I hated the actions and the behavior, but I didn't hate *you*." Anger and resentment filled my soul, turning it black. I needed to escape, not that I had an array of choices or places to go. Muscles quivered in my legs and red-hot anger coursed through my veins, pushing me towards a fight I did not want. Not here. However, my mouth apparently had no control. "You know what, I suppose for a while, I actually did hate you. What you did was unforgiveable."

"Unforgiveable?" His voiced cracked.

"Unforgiveable." I emphasised it just to drive home the deep-seated way he wrecked me, destroyed me. It was a small relief to me how the lights were dim as I didn't need to see a mirrored look of hurt on his face. Yanking my jacket roughly over my arms, I zipped it up to my chin, nearly catching it. "I need a moment."

My civility was waxing, and if he kept bringing it up, I sensed the explosion I should've had years ago would surface tonight and take out him and possibly the other guests sharing space with us. And as angry as I was at Ales, this wasn't the place. We could get trapped back in the before times and reminisce. At least recalling those fond memories would take the sting off. We'd just have to jump over four months of personal hell.

Chapter
EIGHT

I pushed through the west doors and the cool air smacked against my uncovered face. The winds still gusted, and the temperature must've dropped a few more degrees. I pulled myself further into my winter coat and blinked to adjust to the darkness.

Long gone was twilight, which in a small town nestled between huge, towering mountains never lasted very long. It seemed to go from daylight to darkness in a heartbeat.

My eyes watered thanks to the chill, and it took me a moment before I focused on the wooden banister of the boardwalk. The length of it faded into black, and terrified at what roamed out there was enough to give me the heebie-jeebies. The wind whistling against the side of the building didn't help any either.

Instead of venturing too far away, I remained safely close to the door, where enough of an interior glow was present. Rather than stare into the foreboding darkness around me, I turned and peered into the observation area. The subdued guests huddled in small groups of two or three, and all wore the same look of resignation. A low-key card game was going on at one table, and at another, a lady tore into her snack pile. I continued scanning the room until I found Ales.

His head braced against his hands and those shoulders, capable of so much strength, were rolled in. The feet beneath him were flat on the ground but he lifted his heels up and rolled his ankles before setting them down. The motion itself was very rhythmic.

It was mean for me to have said anything, and I chastised myself for being such a total bitch. I should've walked away before I let the words fall out of my mouth. Apparently, ten years of distance didn't heal the wound; it only made it fester. That wasn't fair to Ales, but it also wasn't fair to me. He'd hurt me when he left. No explanation, no reason. He left me to pick up the pieces of my fractured heart. How could I ever forgive him for that? And yes, the anger when he abandoned me was sky high.

I destroyed everything he'd ever given me and tore all our pictures into two. According to my sister, who at thirteen probably wasn't the best person to have listened to, it was key to never have anything around to remind me of what we'd had. Only later, would I regret that rage of destruction, as we'd had so many good times too, and I missed having that special someone who just got me around.

I shuddered as another gust of wind blew through me and caused a creepy whistling in the distance. Yeah, I was done getting some fresh air, and stepped back to the door, pulling it open.

All eyes fixated on me, likely due to the blast of cold air that accompanied me. In my twisted anger and selfishness, I'd forgotten the platform was running on bare bones electrical energy, and the heat was already lowered.

Tony walked by with Jaysen on his heels. Together they were dropping off a blanket or two at each table. I met him where Ales and I were set up.

"Here's a blanket. Sorry there's not enough for everyone, you'll have to share."

Ales and I both stared at each other. Not a thought either of us wanted to entertain.

"Here's a flashlight as well. Again, sorry there's only one for the pair of you."

I picked it up, the weight of it heavy in my hands. "It's okay. No one knew this was going to happen." It's not as if the tram station would have a dozen blankets on hand. These things weren't supposed to have happened to begin with. "But we appreciate it."

The folded blanket sat on the end of the table, and I rested the flashlight on top.

"We've located a kettle in the kitchen and

a box of tea bags. It's not much, but we can fire it up and make a few cups of something warm to drink. I'll be setting that up in the gift station in a couple of minutes."

Those words perked up Ales. "Thanks. A tea would be nice."

My gaze fell to the floor as my shoulders curled over my chest. "Look, about my earlier comment." Betraying my confidence, my voice cracked. "I was out of line, and I apologize."

"I guess I never really understood how my actions affected–"

My finger flew to his lips and covered them. "Please, just stop. We need to get through this night in one piece." I sat back in my chair, remembering the hot chocolate filled thermos inside it. For now, I had something warm and enjoyed the sweet sip of peppermint to coat my throat. I tipped it toward Ales.

"No, thanks, I'll wait for the tea." He shook his head.

"I swear I don't have cooties."

"It's not that." His lopsided smile appeared. "I'm just not thirsty." He pointed to the soda I'd bought him earlier, and the water bottle beside it. "Besides, I have plenty to keep me going, but I intend on pacing myself."

"No lights in the bathroom." I finished his sentence off for him as we both turned toward the hallway leading to the bathroom.

A flashlight beam bounced off the walls.

Tony had mentioned power to the bathroom would be cut off, and the platform was running on bare bones electricity as it was.

I pulled out of my jacket and draped it around the chair next to me.

"What are you doing?"

"This way, when it cools down, I can put my coat on and warm back up." I scrunched my nose at him as it wasn't that cold in the observation area yet. "This is completely backed by science."

"But your jacket will be cold, and it'll take longer to reheat. Just leave your coat on."

Many of the others were in their winter coats, maybe not the accessories, but they weren't messing around. Later though, they'd regret not having another layer to slip on. "Tell you what, I'll sit on it to keep it warm, so then it's ready."

He fingered the edge of the blanket. "And this?"

"If I really need it. I have a hat and a scarf and solid mitts and boots. I should be just fine. Not toasty, but not enough to freeze to death either. Aren't you prepared?"

He checked both sides of the table and shook his head. "I didn't come with a backpack, and I only have this jacket." He ran his hand over the heavy wool coat draped on the chair beside him. "Oh, and a hat and gloves tucked into the pocket."

I ducked under the table to check out his footwear. "You're not even wearing boots." How did he think that was acceptable footwear? It's the Rockies, at the end of winter, for crying out loud. "It gets super cold up on the mountain."

"I wasn't supposed to be up here overnight. I was only coming up for a quick stopover, grab a dinner and be at Stavros' place for nine o'clock." A crushing look settled over his features. "My suitcase is in the car. Down there."

"A lot of good it'll do you up here."

"Right?" He dipped his head beneath the table and surfaced quickly. "You really came prepared."

"I live in town and know how the conditions up here are much colder than down there, how fast the winds can change, and the revolving power failures."

"This whole situation isn't a big deal to you?"

I lifted my shoulders and let them fall. "Not really. I mean it is a big deal in the sense that I'm stranded…" The word was out before I stopped it, and a look into the depths of Ales' eyes confirmed I'd said the wrong word. Immediately, I went over and sat beside him, grabbing his hand. "But if it helps, I'm glad I'm not up here alone."

Scanning the room, there wasn't anyone sitting alone so I'm sure I would've joined up with someone to pass the night. But I didn't know any of these people, and I didn't know if they were trustworthy or not. What if I went to the bathroom and they stole my wallet or my camera? There's nowhere for them to run but nothing's stopping them from tossing my things off the boardwalk into the dark abyss below.

"Hey." A soft finger touched the space between my eyebrows, and I pulled back. "That was some serious thinking you had going on. What's on your mind?"

"It'll sound weird…"

"That's never stopped you before."

"Well, I was thinking how even though you and I aren't much more than, well whatever we are, I know that I'm safe with you."

"I'm happy to hear that. You should know–"

"Don't make statements you aren't able to back up. I can trust you to not steal my stuff, but I don't know about anything beyond that." I gave his hand a gentle squeeze and rose to go back to my side of the table. Suddenly the distance between us was too close, both physically and emotionally. I wasn't *there*, and was pretty sure, I'd never be *there* again.

Ales sighed as I scooted my chair back under the table. "Someday, I hope you'll be able to l–"

The overhead lights above us flickered and Ales and I made eye contact.

"That's not a good sign." Ales glanced around.

The other guests all scanned the ceiling as well.

The lights flickered again and went out.

"Well, damn."

Chapter
NINE

My heart crashed into the floor as the total darkness was blinding. I hated the complete lack of light; it terrified me beyond belief. Always had, always will. At least out on the boardwalk, there was the light from the observation area.

Someone cleared their throat. A flashlight beam danced around, and several other light sources turned on.

"Well, I guess making tea was a bad idea." An unrecognizable voice stated the obvious.

"Yeah, kettles draw a lot of power."

A warm hand wrapped around mine. "You're safe." It was a whisper, intended only for my ears, unlike the other voices muttering in the pale wash of flashlights.

Tony's voice, unmistakable in its strength commanded attention. "Well, folks. It seems like that's the end of our heat and power. Please remain inside as much as you can, although, I should mention, up here, the night skies are incredible and several times a year we have a stargazer's night. If you go out, try to go out in a group as to minimize the heat loss. The interior shouldn't drop below freezing, but it will likely get pretty chilly especially if you're going in and out." A bright light flashed in Tony's direction. "If you head outside, give yourselves a couple of minutes to adapt your eyes, but what you'll see is a thing of beauty. And very few people will see it the way you'll be able."

I leaned across the table. "There's a positive spin for you."

"Want to check it out?"

There was enough light from the other flashlights and cell phones that I wasn't going to turn ours on. Save the battery and all that. Plus, there was something sweet and soft on Ales' face that drew me in like a moth to a flame. He was looking at me like he used to back before we started university, when he wanted to do something wild and crazy, and I was the one to put the brakes on. He wore that same determined expression, as if by saying yes to his plea, it was an unspoken vow of protecting me and keeping me safe. It was hard to say no to.

"Okay."

He let go of my hand and immediately I shuddered as the cooler air rushed over it.

I grabbed my hat and scarf from my bag

and after slipping into my jacket, put them on, tucking my hair under the hat as much as I could. Mitts in hand, I stood beside Ales as he bundled up.

We were just about to depart for the west doors when a lightbulb went off. "Let me set my camera. I'll bet I could take some pretty amazing photos if it's as wonderful as Tony said."

Ales' voice echoed in the small space. "Anyone else want to check out the skies?"

It was met with a silence so deathly quiet, the sound of me changing the dials on my camera was ear splitting.

"Alright, it's just us then."

With a new exposure length set up and the f-stop position ready to go, I made one final adjustment to the ISO rating, but having never taken photographs at night, I wasn't sure how they'd turn out without the use of a tripod. It was going to be a learning experience for sure.

The camera dangled by its strap around my neck as we made out way to the door. Ales had the blanket tucked under his arm in case we got too cold, but I'd suggested at that point we should come back inside. Like always, he disagreed and said we should enjoy as much of it as we could.

The first step back outside was a bitter one. My breath floated and hung in the air, and the blast of cold nipped at the exposed skin, but without the wind blowing, it was actually tolerable. A perk to living in the mountains for years - I acclimated fairly quickly.

Ales, on the other hand, gasped, and a violent shiver wracked his body. "Jesus, it's cold out here."

I smiled beneath the cover of darkness; glad he wasn't able to see my smirk. It didn't ever get that cold in Victoria, and it had been years since he'd lived back in a northern climate and, for a moment, I was laughing at how unprepared he was for the mountain peak.

He hadn't let go of my mitted hand and without a light, we felt our way along the boardwalk.

"Holy shit," he breathed out as we passed beyond the edge of the building, to the bench we'd sat upon earlier in the bright of daylight.

It seemed I was as unprepared for the night skies as he'd been for visiting the summit improperly dressed.

The skies were incredible, and the sight took my breath away. "Ales, look." Under the blanket of more pinpoints of light than I'd ever be able to count, even a whisper felt like a scream.

Ales hadn't moved an inch and lowered his voice to a volume barely registerable. "Would you look at all those stars? There must be a thousand. A million. Even a billion that we can see."

As I scanned the skies there were an infinite amount of tiny pinpricks, bright sparkling stars, and the odd sprinkling of fuzzy patches everywhere. The neatest part was an incredible cluster of white and dark patches stretching across the sky like a healed scar.

"What is that?" I leaned toward Ales as I pointed my mitted hand toward the monstrosity.

"I'm not sure. The Milky Way maybe? I've heard people say they can see it in the total dark." He wrapped his arm around me and planted a quick peck on my cheek. "Happy birthday, Corrine. Make a wish on a shooting star."

I scanned the skies and suddenly there it was – a streak of white highlighted against the velvety blackness. My eyes closed and I made a wish, holding my breath while I pictured my dream.

"You should take some pictures before we freeze to death." His breath was warm against my ear, enough to cause it to glow.

"Yes," I breathed out. "Pictures."

It almost seemed like the stars were giving off enough light to navigate us as my eyes didn't struggle to see through the inky blanket of darkness.

I unhooked my camera and kneeled on the boardwalk, using the banister as a steady edge. Making a few minor adjustments, I snapped some pictures and checked out what I'd taken on the screen, which blinded me with its brightness. Didn't matter, they were all blurry. I wasn't able to hold still enough to get a decent pic without a tripod. Too bad, as the skies were definitely something I wanted photographic proof of.

Instead, I walked back toward the tram side

of the building and stared over the edge. My home was down below, a sea of glittering lights in a forest of black. That was worthy of a photograph and I re-aimed my camera to capture the sights below. I'd never seen a picture of my town at night from so high above. It was magical and majestic. As I aimed for the main platform station, my camera turned off. The cold had zapped the battery power.

"Well, there goes that."

"Camera died?"

"Sure did." But I wasn't in a hurry to go back inside and put it away. I could stand to be outside for a few minutes more, so I unzipped the top part of my jacket and slipped the camera in, along with a cold gust of air. My body heat should keep the camera protected once I warmed back up and until I tucked it back into my bag.

"Want to sit for a minute?"

I did.

He reached for my hand and led us over to the bench, sitting on the side furthest away from the door. The skies above continued to impress. Ales snuggled in against me and draped the blanket over our legs. It was such a wild contrast as instantly I felt warm again.

We were the only ones outside, and as much as I wanted to shout to the other guests in the observation area about what they were missing, I also didn't want to leave Ales' side. It bothered me how comfortable I was with him after all this time, and how in return he was the same with me.

"Corrine, I want to tell you something." He held me tight, but I didn't fight it. "I need to apologize. All those years ago, I was a dumb fuck, and I did some stupid things."

I twisted, pulling away just enough to feel the coolness between our shoulders. Under the starlight, I made out his profile. Like before, I put my mitted hand over his lips, but this time, he pulled it away.

"No. I need to say this."

My heart throbbed loud enough for Ales to hear it, and a tightness surrounded my chest and started squeezing.

"I shouldn't have left."

A low laugh rolled off my dry lips. "I never blamed you for leaving. You got a scholarship to UBC. By spring break in our high school year, I knew you were going there."

"I mean after."

I knew that's what he meant, but I wasn't ready to go there. Even after all this time. I bit the edge of my lip while trying to concentrate on his face. "Oh, right."

After university began. That fall, he left for the University of British Columbia in Vancouver, and I stayed behind, renting a place with four others within walking distance of my university. As promised, Ales came home for Thanksgiving, and again after Christmas, where he stayed with me as my roommates went home for the holidays.

We were the perfect couple. Just the two of us, in our own place, loving each other with abandon. And it was everything we dreamed of. We talked about post-graduation and where we'd live, and all the crazy things people blinded by love discuss. We planned and dreamed. Our future all marked out.

Until…

I started feeling off and nauseous like I'd never experienced before. At the beginning of February, my later than normal period had still failed to arrive, so I took a pregnancy test. Those two lines were not expected, and I took a test daily until Ales came home for reading week at the end of February. Over dinner one night, I announced the news and showed him the tests to prove it. Based on when we were last together, I'd be having a baby, our baby, in September. I wouldn't be returning to university, and with a child on the way, neither would he. Our planned future went up in smoke.

Distraught, he was instantly mad and angry, and hurtful words flew between us, although most were flung in my direction. He left that night, and never came back. But that wasn't the worst of it.

His arm tightened around me, and his body shook against mine. "I'm sorry, Corrine. I'm sorry I didn't come back. I was a jerk. I just didn't know it then like I know it now."

His pleading tone and words sliced open

the weak stitches I had made in repairing my heart and caused a ten-year build up of tears to burst forth like a dam breaking free. "You have no idea how much you hurt me. I needed you when I went into the hospital, but you wouldn't return my calls." I pushed away, and my hand jerked through the air, ready to connect with something. A sharp pain rippled through my chest and a surge of red-hot anger grew like flames in the wind.

A few weeks after I had informed Ales of his impending fatherhood, the unthinkable happened. During class I had the worst cramps and started throwing up. My friend hauled me over the hospital where I was told what was happening – I was losing my baby. I called and called Ales, only getting his voicemail.

Tears fell harder and my vision blurred. In the depths of my mitts, I curled my nails into my palm and squeezed with all my might. "I've never needed anyone as much as I needed you then. There was nothing you could've done, except hold me, and that was all I wanted and craved. I wanted to tell you your dreams were still alive, even if mine were dying." Frozen lips splintered as I pinched them together. My body shook as it remembered laying on the hospital bed in the emergency room completely alone, hating my damaged body. "Jules snuck out of school to come and get me and take me back to my place. To this day, I've never told my parents."

"You haven't?" His voice cracked.

My quivering chin fell to my chest, only to be stopped by my scarf. Shame was a horrible emotion, and for years, I'd held on to the disgrace of being so broken. "Oh, they knew we'd split up. I had to move back home as I couldn't work, I couldn't attend classes, I couldn't function. I died the day you left me, but when we lost the baby and you never returned my calls, I became all dead. You can ask Jules, although she'd likely kill you as to see you again."

He shuddered beneath me and pulled the blanket up higher.

"Oh, Corrine, I'm so sorry. Like I said I was a jerk. But I did listen to all your messages. I have no explanation for my behaviour. I was just mad that you'd gotten pregnant and hadn't told me for so long. That hurt."

"I didn't get pregnant on my own, and I couldn't tell you over the phone. I wanted to tell you in person, but you weren't coming home for another three weeks."

"I understand that now, but back then…"

Tears froze like icicles on my cheeks and I shook like a leaf, even though it wasn't from the cold. Staying in the same spot, I folded my hands onto my lap. "Like I said, I hated the actions, but only learned that when my parents threw me into therapy."

"Jesus, you saw a shrink?"

"Had to." Not a fine moment in my life, but there wasn't any option. I had simply ceased to exist, I was there in body, but my spirit was gone. "She said it was going to take some time to heal, to process, to move on and to forgive."

"I'm afraid to ask, but how long did that take?"

"I still haven't moved on, and forgiveness is asking way too much."

"There's never been another man in your life?"

I shook my head. "Not a serious one." I grimaced. Too afraid I'd give my heart for them to abandon me when I needed them the most. Sure, I'd date, but it was superficial and after a couple of dinners, I just knew it wasn't going to work. "They were never you, and despite how much you hurt me, I still had feelings for you."

He squeezed me harder. "Oh, Corrine."

"How fast did you get over me?" It was probably lightning quick.

"Depends on who you ask. Stavros would say it never happened, but Billy, my best friend, would say I was playing the field soon enough after we broke up."

"Is that what you told your friends? That we broke up, and not that you left me?" He was the one to walk away, to destroy all that we had. Whereas Ales had been my whole life, apparently, I'd been a minor bump in his.

"I never gave the circumstances of our split to anyone, well, except Stav. He knew."

Of course, he would've confided in him;

they were close.

He leaned in and wiggled in his seat. "But the field wasn't right and every girl I dated had the same issue."

The words choked me. "And what was that?"

"They weren't you. All of them got measured against the one I had loved, and they failed."

Chapter
TEN

My mouth fell open and my eyes widened. After all these years, Ales harboured feelings for me. It was unbelievable, but still caused a fluttery sensation deep in my belly. "There wasn't a special lady? Not ever? In ten years?"

"No one worth holding onto." He tipped his head to the side as the corners of his eyes rounded up. "Why do you find that hard to believe?" There was a smidgen of smugness in his voice.

"Because you're you."

He removed a glove and touched the side of my face, warming the icicles on my cheek and melting the ice on my heart. "And I could say the same about you. There's been no one? At all?"

It was sad, but true. I hadn't been truly intimate with anyone since Ales. My shrink said when the person ready to hold my heart and cherish it for the gift it was, I would know it, and I'd be willing to be with him. I was finally ready to give a part of my heart to someone. "Noah." His name slipped off my tongue.

"Who's Noah?" He tightened under me.

I shrugged and pulled away. The blanket slipped off my thighs and instantly, a coldness settled over me. "This guy I'm sort of seeing."

"Sort of? How does *sort of* work?" There was a terseness in his speech, and hearing it threw me for a loop.

My chin fell and I pulled my toque lower over my ears. "Well, we go out for dinner and hang out, and haven't moved beyond second base. Tonight was going to be a special dinner, aside from it being my birthday and all. I was going to tell him I was ready to commit and move on with him in my life."

A warm blast of air sailed by, followed by a sad sigh. "Except you gave up your ticket to stay up here with me."

A tightness filled my chest. "Yeah, something like that. But we weren't actually supposed to be here overnight. Just for a couple more hours, right?" Like everything else in my life, nothing went according to plan. When was I ever going to learn that?

"I'm sorry. Again." The regret was thick in his tone.

"Well, at least neither of us is alone up here." I'd rather spend my birthday up here with him than in a town all alone, like I had in previous years. Sighing at the way things turned out, I twisted back to sit beside him and leaned against him like it was the most natural thing in the world.

A subtle, contented sigh breathed out of him. "Is it wrong if I tell you I'm glad you're with me?"

I didn't want to answer him. I didn't have the answer myself. "I'm getting chilled, and I'm going in."

* * *

Walking back into the observation area, my heart felt lighter than it had in years. I'd said what I needed to say, and somehow, I'd kept it civil. Mostly. Maybe that was part of moving on. As much as the whole situation had ruined me, I was able to talk about it, cry over it, and put some distance between us. Much had been said. He'd admitted how he'd never found another to fill his heart, just maybe someone to satisfy his carnal needs, according to his buddy. It was a small comfort to know I wasn't the only one who'd been aching, but why had he never reached out to me? Even a few years later? Probably because I would've ignored him and ran as fast as my legs would've carried me.

Yet, here we were, stuck together at the top of a mountain, sharing space with thirteen others in the pitch black with no heat. Thank goodness I had snacks and drinks to get me through to the morning.

The low lighting of a few flashlights gave us just enough visibility to make our way back over to our table.

"Y'all need to check that out. Seriously amazing," Ales announced once we were back inside the observation area.

As I tucked the camera back into the bag, I pulled out the thermos, twisting off the cap. The drink was lukewarm at best, but it was sweet, and it hit the spot, warming up the back of my throat which I didn't even know could get cold. I offered some to Ales.

"I'll stick to my pop, thanks." He took a fizzy drink, the noise of the escaping gas filling the area and silencing the guests.

I started shivering while the chairs across the room scraped across the floor and tried to pace it off in hopes it would create some internal heat.

"You okay?" Ales got up close and personal.

"I'm cold."

"We're inside now. You'll warm up." He ran his gloved hands over my shoulders.

Stupid me forgot how long warming back up sometimes took. It was rare for me to shiver from the cold when I was outside, but lately, after a minute or two in warmer quarters, my body would suddenly start shaking, sometimes uncontrollably. Typically, a hot shower, or better yet a hot bath, would warm me up, but I had none of that at my disposal. I tugged my hat down lower and pulled my arms out of my sleeves and pressed them into my chest. My teeth chattered as I squatted down to the ground and curled against the wall. The air inside the observation area was much warmer than outside, but to my body it didn't seem to matter.

"Jesus, you really are cold." He dropped down in front of me. "Come here." He unbuttoned his coat. "Lean against me. I'm warm."

It was enough to rest against him outside where a few thick inches of material separated us. No way was I going to crawl into his jacket and press myself to him with only his and my sweater between our skins.

"Come on, you're being ridiculous."

"I'm being cautious. Nothing can happen between us. We're over. Done. The air has been cleared and all that." The light in the corner where we were was minimal and the table shielded any remaining.

Ales reached up and grabbed the blanket, draping it around me and pulling me close as I shivered. He looked me in the eye as he dropped his gloves onto the floor beside him and slowly reached up to touch my face. "See, I'm nice and warm."

His touch lit a fire in me, not one strong enough to warm me up, but still it was sweet to have his fingers on my cheek again. He had always been the one to mass produce the heat, where I had always been the one to suck it up. His fingers moved slowly from my face over to the zipper on my jacket, where he lifted the toggle and moved it down my chest successfully opening my coat. His gaze never left mine. Gently, he lifted each of my legs, placing each one on either side of his hips and pulled me closer, closing the gap between us in a heartbeat. He pushed his hands around my back and guided me toward his chest, and when my cheek was pressed against the warm sweater he had on, he shifted the blanket to wrap tightly around me.

All at once, I was comforted and starting to warm up.

It was also the closest I've been to sex in years, and I was stunned it was with Ales because never in a million years had I pictured us back together.

Regardless of my feelings, the need to warm up won over my need for physical distancing. I closed my eyes and breathed him in, inhaling a mixture of a spicy scent and an outdoor woodsy smell. It was calming and relaxing, and I drifted off from time to time.

I snapped back when something clattered to the floor. It was too dark to see, and I tightened my grip on Ales.

"It's okay, it was just a flashlight."

Ales had his hands wrapped around my back, but they were under the blanket as it fluttered to the floor.

"What time is it?" I rubbed my eyes. They

were dry since my contacts were still in and seriously needed eye drops. As I stretched, a rush of cool air snuck in between us, and it was then I noticed how toasty warm I had become and how my shivering had ceased.

Ales checked his phone, and I shielded my eyes from the harshness. "It's after midnight."

Only a few more hours to go until daylight broke, and the helicopters arrived to take us back home. I could do this.

"Do you want anything to drink?" He reached up to the table to grab his pop and take a sip.

"I'm good." Until I heard him chug back more than a gentle sip. "Sure." I wrapped my hand around his as he passed me the bottle. Years ago, it would've electrified me and sent tingles pulsating up to my heart, but suddenly it felt natural. Comfortable. Perfectly Ales. I took a lady-sized sip and gave him back his bottle.

A shudder coursed through me.

"Come here." He patted his chest for good measure.

"I can't. I just can't."

"Sure, you can." He stared into the depths of me, those dark eyes searching for acceptance. "You did it before."

"Yes, when it was needed."

"But we both needed it, and still do. It's going to be a long, cold night and the only way we'll make it through is to…" He inhaled sharply,

puffing out his chest. "Is to stick close together."
He meant snuggle, but there was more weight to
those words than either of us wanted to hear.
Repositioning himself, he scooted closer to the
wall. "Come on, you know I don't bite."

"Fine." I resigned myself to his comfort,
but it wasn't going to change anything. Inching
across the cool floor, I pressed in between his legs
where I could lean against the corner of the wall if
Ales' strong chest wasn't comfortable enough. But
his sweater was nicer to lean on, softer and more
forgiving. I placed my head against his pecs and
tugged my hat down a little lower.

Ales pulled the blanket over us, tucking it
between my shoulders and him. Naturally, his hand
rubbed my back, the motion at once soothing any
frazzled nerves I may have had.

It was oddly quiet in the observation area.
Sleepy voices floated through the air, but they were
incoherent to my ears. Across the space, a gentle
snore rippled, and outside, the wind gently
caressed the windows. Definitely a less than ideal
circumstance and yet, no one was scared or going
mad. It was a calm situation.

"What are things like back home?" I tipped
my head back to look up into Ales' face, but he
kept staring outward.

"They're good."

"Do you love your job?"

"With all my heart."

"That's important you know. It gives a

sense of purpose." At least that's what my friends told me. *Find a job you love, and you'll never work a day in your life,* or something like that.

"What about you? You like yours?" His hand ran down my back.

"I hate it, but it pays the bills. I'm hoping the pictures I take from here will be helpful and get me on the right path."

"What about your engineering degree?"

My wavering smile diminished, and my words were muffled by his sweater. "I never finished."

"Say that again?"

I inhaled sharply and exhaled slowly. "I never finished."

"What? Why not?"

"Because of how things ended between us and the baby. After that all happened, I had no desire to finish up. Plus, I'd missed all my finals."

"Because of me, right?"

It wasn't all his fault, even if to this day my parents blamed Ales for my dropping out. Sure, maybe he could've come home and been with me for a bit while I recovered, or perhaps responded to my calls. Or maybe not have acted so rashly when I told him the news. Angry tears threatened to slip out.

"I'm sorry, Corrine." He rubbed my arm and held me tightly.

"Why did you walk away? That's one thing you've never answered to."

His heart raced beneath my ear, the pumping of it strong and steady. "You'd never understand."

"Try me." Tears overflowed their holds and snaked their way down my cheeks.

"I was scared. When you said you were…?" His voiced dropped so low I barely heard it, which also meant anyone else listening couldn't hear either. "You were pregnant, I didn't believe it. We'd been so careful."

"I know. You'd mentioned that, that horrible night before you stormed away."

"And I was afraid for our future, the one we'd planned, and suddenly, that all went up in smoke. Gone. My next year was done, as I'd have to find a full-time job and drop out. My career was finished before it even had a chance, and I was angry about that."

"So was I."

"I couldn't talk to you for a while, as I was trying to figure things out. I wasn't sleeping, my schoolwork suffered, and I was getting ready to throw in the hat, so to speak. One night, I looked up to the stars and wished you'd never gotten pregnant; that it was a terrible thing to have happened and to have it come between us like it had. A week later, you called to tell me the bad news." His voice cracked. "I figured it was because of me that you mis… that you lost the baby, and I couldn't face you again. To think I'd ruined your future, our future, and then wanted the worst to happen to erase it. I'm a horrible, horrible person." He swiped a hand across his face. "But I didn't really want that, I just wanted an easy escape, the easy answer. I'm so sorry for wishing for something like that. Could you ever forgive me?"

It had been a question my shrink asked constantly. At what point would I be willing to forgive Ales? Just as I wasn't sure then, I was just as confused now. I didn't know what to say or do. I was frozen in my spot, listening to him cry, feeling the heave of his chest as the torment rolled through him, and I wanted him to hurt. At least for a little bit.

Chapter
ELEVEN

I wished I could say I let him cry for hours, days, weeks even, but I didn't. I couldn't bear to let him hurt the way I'd been hurt and hearing him weep undid all the anger in me and sent it unraveling to the floor. Besides, Ales wasn't a crier, his father claimed it made him a weaker man, so for him to be openly hurting like that, I knew his heartache was nearly matched to my own.

"Oh, Ales." I angled my body toward him and placed my hands on either side of his cheeks. His beard was damp, and my heart splintered a bit further. "You weren't the cause of it. I swear."

"But I'm evil for ever having wished it, because it came true."

"It wasn't your fault."

"But still…"

His chest heaved and I found myself pressing into him a little harder. Unable to make proper contact comfortably, I twisted myself around and put my legs on either side of him, so we were chest to chest. My arms braced on his shoulders and I held his face tightly between my hands, although it was difficult to make contact in the hovering darkness. "Listen to me." I stared into those sorrowful eyes. "It happened. It was no one's fault, sometimes these things just don't work out."

"But I ruined you."

"Yeah, you did."

He closed his eyes, and a warm wetness touched my thumb.

"I'm working on getting over it. Being here with you is helping. We're voicing all the things I desperately wanted and needed all those years ago." And it was true. Finally, deep down, that pain, that hurt, it was fading away.

With that, he made eye contact with me. "I'm so sorry."

I nodded. "I know."

"I never wanted to hurt you."

A grimace wore through my defences and a shrug rolled down my back. I'd always wondered the motive behind his lack of communication and now, I had it. I thought my body would be angrier or lash out and induce enough physical pain to mimic the hell I went through. Instead, I leaned in closer and touched my lips to his.

I breathed him in and held him tight, as if he were the only air I had access to. He responded and reciprocated, parting his lips, and welcoming me home. Like no time had passed between us, we were connected on a physical level devoid in our lives for nearly a decade.

I plunged my tongue into the depths of his mouth, searching and tangling myself in him. My hands dropped from his cheeks to his neck, where they wrapped around his back as I flattened my breasts against him. We were lip locked and tongue tied, and it was perfect, natural and the best way to reconnect. His hands ran up my arms, the palm grazing the side of my breasts on their journey north, although I would've been satisfied with a southern move too. Long fingers wove themselves under my hat and into my hair, gently breaking us apart so he could trail kisses down my cheeks, over my throat, and burying his nose in the top of my sweater, leaving me breathless with anticipation.

I tipped my head back up and kissed across his whiskery face, over to his ear, licking and sucking his lobe. It still had the same effect as between us; a hardness formed under his pants and a low throaty groan rolled out of him. I tried to stifle it, to silence it even, but I failed and from across the room someone snickered. We weren't the only ones awake.

Damn.

I rested my forehead on his shoulder and placed my hand over the incessant pounding of his heart. "I'm sorry. I got carried away." It was a whisper quiet enough I hoped only Ales heard.

His jagged breath blew in my ears. "I would've stopped us. I don't have a condom."

"Neither do I." There were other things we could've done, but given our surroundings and circumstances, it was a good thing we were interrupted. Even if it would take a while to put out the flames.

He leaned back against the wall with a sigh and I curled into him. Once again, he wrapped the blanket around us, trapping in the heat we were giving off in waves.

I rested my head on his chest, my ear to his heart and listened, matching my breathing to its speed. Slowly it returned to a normal beating rhythm, and I assumed by the even breaths moving his chest, that Ales had fallen asleep.

How I wished I could do the same. After that encounter, a million thoughts swirled in my head – the main question being, what the hell happens now? Do we go our separate ways tomorrow? He goes to Stavros's wedding, and I go back to my mundane life? Our living situation would need to be dealt with if anything did start up. But what about his life? What about mine? And what of Noah? I know we weren't exclusive, but I'd been at the point where I wanted us to be, until this. If given a choice between the two, who would I-?

Alessandro.

The name rolled out of me before I could even finish my thought. That was who I wanted, but did he want me the same way? What if I put myself out there again and he said it wouldn't work? I didn't know if I'd be able to handle a second rejection. And besides, in reality, it never worked.

No, it was best to just ride out the night and the early morning and watch him leave. I could handle that. I had to.

Chapter
TWELVE

I woke up beside Ales, wrapped in his arms. My movement startled him, and he jerked in response.

"Just me," I said, pushing myself into a sitting position. Even if I had been safe in Ales' embrace, I most definitely was not sleeping in the most comfortable position. My body groaned and creaked with each motion, and my neck had the most awful kink to it. I pinched the tight muscles as Ales sat up.

"That was some night."

It was like a dream, but now in the dawn of morning, I wondered how much had actually been in my head? Had we finally said what we'd been holding onto all these years? To me, the air was clearer, and the future not so black and white.

The blanket fluttered off me, and I raced to snatch it before it hit the floor. It was mighty crisp in the observation area, and I swore I saw puffs of breath hanging in the air. The sun hadn't yet crested the mountain peaks and streamed into the room, but the fresh wash of morning was approaching.

The other guests remained still and lifeless, although someone was snoring.

Keeping my voice low, I asked, "Want to watch the sun rise?" I rifled through my bag, hoping to find a spare battery for the camera. Usually there was one in there somewhere.

He rubbed his face and stretched, and quickly huddled back together. "Jesus, it's cold."

"I know." I took off my hat and gave my matted hair a fluff, thinking it may help to trap more heat. My mitts had become a makeshift pillow and to test them out I slipped my hands into them. Ah, still warm. "It's been a long time since we watched the sun rise together."

After high school graduation, we partied until the sun came up, which in our neck of the woods was around 4:30 a.m., although by time reading week rolled around, and he was home, the sun rose later at 8. Much nicer.

"Sure, what the hell." He stood and stretched again, giving me an unobstructed view of his toned abs. Someone still did his daily workouts. My own had fallen to the wayside. That's not to say I let myself go, but I wasn't as dedicated as I used to be. After reaching high, he extended a hand down to me and helped me onto my feet.

I lost my footing and stumbled into him,

gazing up into his sleepy face. "Sorry." I didn't know what else to say. "Do you want some breakfast?"

He rubbed his chin and looked at me thoughtfully. "Sure, eggs benedict would be great."

I laughed, keeping my voice low. However, the others in the area were starting to stir. "Well then, once we get down to the main station, there's a place in town that makes the best eggs benedict. Eggs Athabee. And they are to die for."

That brought a smile to his face. "Maybe later."

I grabbed a bag of peanuts. "Until then, will this suffice?"

"It's protein, sure."

We each choked down a handful, chasing it with a swig of warm soda – not an ideal breakfast, but under the circumstances, it had to do.

The rest of the bag fell into my pocket before I zipped up my jacket. "Shall we?" I looped the camera over my neck and pulled out my flattened, in-desperate-need-of-a-wash hair.

"Yes, let's go."

We tiptoed over to the doors and as quickly as possible, exited the building, trying not to let in too much cool air. But the outside air took my breath away, and I tugged up my scarf to cover my mouth and nose.

"Much colder than last night, eh?"

Ales had buttoned his jacket right to the top and his green scarf covered his face too.

"C'mon."

The sky was getting brighter with the morning sun, and if my prediction was correct, it was going to crest the northern side of Mount Tekerra. If I hurried, I'd be able to capture that first break of dawn, a new experience and a first for me.

"C'mon," I called out over my shoulder as I stepped off the boardwalk and made my way over the crunching snow. The wind from both the gusts and the helicopter had smoothed out the surface and made it quite firm to walk on. As I approached the helicopter landing area, the strut marks were still visible. A neat photo op, so I clicked a few.

Ales was just steps behind me, and we hadn't gone very far away from the boardwalk when I turned the camera to the east and hunched down. The sun was just ready to show off and I made it just in time.

I clicked away, praying that the battery had enough juice to last through the sunrise and our imminent descent back into the warmth of the building. It all had to be photographed.

The sunrise did not disappoint. As it rose, the mountain peak eclipsed it just as the shutter snapped. Somehow, with a little luck, I got the million-dollar shot. Ales stood beside me, teeth chittering away, and in a flash, I pointed the camera at him and got a few candid pics before he noticed.

"Hey," he called out. "The sun is that way." But there was a smile big enough to push his cheeks above his scarf line.

I resumed capturing the morning sun and tucked the camera back against my chest. I retrieved my cell phone and held out the camera. "Care for a selfie?"

Ales leaned in and lowered his scarf. I fluffed the ends of my hair and allowed the gentle morning breeze to do their thing. We looked cold and tired, but happy.

"A fresh start," he said.

There was a hidden meaning in his words, no doubt. It wasn't just the sunrise or the long, passionate kiss last night or the opening of our hearts. It was like we were getting a do over.

"Hurry up, I'm freezing."

We leaned in, and I took a picture or two before repocketing it. I needed the remaining battery power to touch base with friends when I was back at the main station.

"Send that to me."

"You'll have to give me your number first."

"When we're back in there." He tipped his head to the upper tram station a couple hundred feet away.

The sunlight blanketed the area in its brilliance, the packed snow glittering like the stars in the sky had last night. If I believed hard enough, it was warm enough to take the edge off the cold. Of course, it was all an illusion, and I was drunk with a lack of sleep, but still I believed, and for whatever reason, I didn't want this moment to end.

"Want to build a snowman?"

"How horribly offended would you be if I said no?"

"Horribly." I laughed out loud and started walking ahead of him.

During our last hookup before things went south, the snow had been perfect, and in the park near my apartment we'd built the biggest snowman. Even a week later, it was still standing, untouched and undestroyed by neighbourhood hooligans. However, the snow at the top of Whistler's Peak was not the right condition to make snowballs with, let alone a full-sized snowman. Maybe if the sun continued to beat all day and the temps rose above freezing, it would be feasible. Deep down though, I was stalling. I knew what was coming.

"Another time. Promise."

I stopped in my tracks. Ales didn't hand out promises like candy. They meant something to him, and I found myself nodding in agreement.

He wrapped his mitted hand around mine and pulled me at a brisk pace back to the building. As we approached the door, he stopped, and I snuggled in close.

There were long lingering gazes in the sunlight as we made eye contact. The dark green flecks in his eyes were lighter, like leaves in the shade, and I was unable to look away. How had I forgotten the way his irises looked in the morning light? They were mesmerizing.

Put under their spell, I leaned in for a kiss

that did not disappoint. Despite the cold, my cheeks seared from the passion and power in his lips; a kiss that radiated the heat from my core to the tips of my fingers. There would be no worries about me ever freezing to death if he kept kissing me like that.

Sadly, he pulled back. "On three?"

Maybe my kissing skills needed work as they didn't warm him up the way they did me. After his quick countdown, we breezed on it, making sure the door was tightly closed behind us. He held my hand as we entered the observation area.

A few of the other ten guests were still lying on the floor or camped across a table, while a couple of others were pacing around holding their backs or stretching. I think it was safe to say, everyone would sleep better tonight in a real bed where it was much warmer than the current situation.

Tony was up, sitting on the counter in the gift shop with his ear to the phone and his back to us, his two employees standing by, looking worse for wear with bags bigger than my backpack under their eyes. Everyone needed a strong coffee and a warm meal.

Based on Tony's head bobs, it shouldn't be much longer, and our rescue would arrive, but a small part of me wasn't looking forward to it either.

I packed up my camera and tidied up our area, not that we made any mess. As I glanced around, the area was fairly clean and only a few tables were moved and would need to be rearranged. On the whole, I was impressed; everyone kept a level head despite the less than ideal circumstances.

Tony hopped off the counter and stood in front of it, holding up a piece of paper. "Alright. The pilots are at the main station and are prepping for the remaining rescues. They'll use one helicopter, so it'll be about a thirty-minute span between rides. Our first flight will include…"

As luck would have it, Ales and I were on the first flight with five others. The second flight carried the next five, and the final flight included the two staff and Tony, who would lock up.

"The first flight will be taking off shortly, so please gather up your things and be ready."

I looked out the observation window to the valley far below, searching for the waiting helicopter. There was nothing visible, so I unpacked my camera for a final check.

Zooming in with the telephoto, there she was in all her glory, but her rotor blades hadn't yet started moving. For good measure, I snapped a few more pictures. The book would be filled with amazing photos, at least I hoped. In addition to the silent chopper, I took a few more pics of the waiting area, capturing the rawness of the situation, knowing hope was on the way.

Without a fond farewell, the battery died, ending my photo session.

"Well, after this, I'm on cell camera." Which sucked. The quality wasn't nearly the same, but at this point it would have to do. I hadn't planned an overnight visit, but looking over at Ales, who was looking at me, I'd say it was worth it.

I walked over and pulled out a chair, needing just a few more minutes and moments with him. "So, after…"

He gave me a solemn nod. "After."

A large inhale of cooled air filled my lungs. "What now?"

It was subtle, but there was a small shake of his head. "I don't know."

"Do we just go back to what we were before yesterday?" *Please say no.*

His lips pursed together. "It's complicated, and there are no easy answers."

"There's not." I sighed and leaned against him. "For what it's worth, I'll be forever thankful for last night."

He gave me a squeeze. "Me too." There was sadness in his voice. "And maybe that's a good thing. Now we can both move on."

That would be the best thing – to move on. We cleared the air, settled a few things, perhaps even mended a few heartaches. But I wanted more. I wanted a do over. A second chance.

The phone rang, making me jump out of Ales' embrace.

Tony picked up the phone, a smile crossing

his face. The short conversation over, he proclaimed, "The helicopter is warming up. It'll be here in less than ten minutes."

My magical night was officially ending.

Chapter
THIRTEEN

The room was alive as the other guest bustled about and chairs scraped across the hardwood floors as they were put back in their places. Blankets were folded and set on the table nearest the gift shop along with several flashlights.

I cleared off our table, pocketing the remaining snacks and drinks into a flapped pocket on side of my bag and hoisted it over my shoulder. Double checking I wasn't leaving anything behind, aside from my mending heart, I headed over to the east doors to await the helicopter as it loudly made its appearance.

"Alright, first flight." Tony stood at the door, peeking out and watching.

"Thanks for everything, Tony." I extended my hand.

He pumped it in return. "I hope this doesn't prevent you from coming back."

"On the contrary, I can't wait to return." I

beamed. "And bring my friends."

"Thank you." Perhaps he'd been nervous that this whole situation would reflect badly on him, but if anything, I hoped it elevated his status. He was a cool cucumber, and I intended on writing a positive letter on his behalf to the higher ups.

Ales shook his hand as well and the roar from the rotors became deafening.

"Good luck to you." With that, he opened the door, and we made our way to the side of the building, awaiting further instructions from the flight crew.

This was it.

I was finally going to have a helicopter ride, and in my excitement, I reached for Ales' hand. It was impossible to contain my smile.

Ales too had a mile-wide grin on his face.

The black helicopter appeared on our left, rising above the tree line, and moving toward the back of the building to the small, flat clearing. It twisted slightly, setting down on its skids. The blades kept rotating as the door on the far side opened, and the pilot or co-pilot hunkered down and made his way over to where the seven of us stood in expectation.

"Alright folks. We're hot loading the chopper so let's make this quick." Although it was loud outside, his voice was clear. "I'll need all your weights and approximate weights of your cargo." He glanced down the line. "Two too many. You two," he pointed at the two nearest the door, "Back inside. You'll be on the next flight."

The last two opened the door and disappeared inside the observation area.

The co-pilot stood in front of each of us and scratched down the numbers given to him and he stared at the list. "There are five seats, two in the middle travelling backwards numbered one and two, and three along the back, numbered three through five. You'll need to sit the way I've assigned you." He glanced back at his sheet and pointed with his pen at each of us, giving us a seat number.

Ales was seat three and I was seat four.

"Let's go. Keep your head down and follow me exactly."

The no mess around pilot led us out to the landing area, and I kept my head lowered, pulling my ears as deep into my jacket as I could. If I thought it was loud before, approaching the running helicopter was ten times louder. We filed into our seats and he slammed the door once Ales was in, running around the front to hop into the seat in the cockpit.

I strapped myself in, watching as Ales did the same. One by one, the passengers were ready to go.

Ales held my hand and whispered, but I was terrible at reading lips and had no idea what he said.

I shook my head, so he leaned over and yelled in my ear. "Now you get to be Caitlyn."

Caitlyn O'Shannessy, the red-headed, feisty co-pilot from *Airwolf*, a tv show from the 80's that Ales and I binge watched on demand. It was a cheesy drama, but I'd often said I wanted to be her. Guess this was as close as I was going to get. And the best part? I was riding with my Stringfellow Hawk. I gave his hand a squeeze as the rotor sound pitched higher and my gut hit the floor as we lifted off and tipped forward.

The colour fell out of Ales' face, so I held his hand even tighter, entwining my fingers through his. We rose into the air, above the tops of the evergreens and started our descent. Our temporary lodgings were visible out the right-side windows as we dropped into the valley. I felt as if I were on a rollercoaster that was constantly freefalling, it was the weirdest feeling. My stomach rolled and rolled, and an irksome worry covered the joy I was supposed to be experiencing. Instead of being thrilled, I was consumed with not getting sick. Guess I was never going to be a full-fledged Caitlyn after all.

The lower platform station came into view, a sight for weary eyes. The other guests in the tight cabin smiled with relief. The chopper descended further and circled the area, coming to land in a vacated part of the mostly deserted parking lot. With a gentle bump, we were on the ground. The whole flight was less than a few minutes.

The door in the front popped open and once again, the co-pilot raced around to open the door beside Ales. We unbuckled and exited, keeping our heads ducked as he led us over to the platform station where we originally took off in the tram, less than twenty-four hours ago. With a quick nod, he bid us adieu and ran back to his waiting ride.

Shielding my eyes, I tucked my head into the crook of my arm as the helicopter blades started spinning extra fast. Holding Ales' hand, the chopper lifted off the ground and took off eastward, avoiding the tram cables. With our rescue vehicle gone and the temperature so much warmer than where we came from, I removed my mitts and hat, and tousled my mangy mess.

Behind us, people filed out of the small building, and headed in our direction.

Ales was as green as I felt. "You going to be okay?"

The little head bob was barely reassuring. "And that was a good flight. No wind gusts."

True. Today was a relatively calm day compared to yesterday.

"And you? You okay?"

"For the most part."

Some of the reporters headed to the others we flew down with, but a couple headed straight to us. Their cameras clicked upon approach and the questions came out of left field.

"Were you scared?"

"Did you think you were going to die up on the mountain?"

"How did you spend your time?"

I plastered on a fake smile and sighed. "The staff, Tony, Gwen and Jaysen were remarkable at keeping us well taken care of. At no point was my life ever in jeopardy, and no, I was never scared. That's all I'm going to say about that for now." Quickly, I turned to Ales, catching a familiar face hanging in the background.

They shoved the camera in Ales' face as I let go of his hand.

"What about you?"

Ales shook his head but looked longingly into my eyes. "I have no comment on the situation."

The reporters continued to ask questions but seeing as they weren't getting the answers they desired, they walked over to the others and waited for the next incoming flight.

As they departed, Noah walked over and without a word wrapped me up in his arms. "Oh, Corrine. I was so worried. When I checked my messages, I'll admit I was unbelieving, but I called the tram station and they verified it for me. Are you okay?"

"I'm okay." Better than okay, but that was neither here nor there.

Ales was checking out Noah and stepped back to give us some space.

"Thankfully, I knew someone up there and he helped to pass the time with me."

No one within eyesight would've missed the solid once over Noah gave Ales. They were both the same height, but Ales had a leaner build whereas Noah was thicker in the shoulders and thighs. His presence alone was commanding enough but the subtle daggers he shot at Ales were red hot.

Noah cleared his throat. "Well, thank you for keeping my girl entertained." He placed his arm around my shoulders and steered me away. "Tell me all about your adventure as you sit in my nice warm truck. Do you want some gum?" He produced a mint flavoured package.

My breath must've been horrid, especially since it'd had been over twenty-fours hours since they last had a good scrubbing. I nodded enthusiastically. "Please." I broke the blister packaging and popped one into my mouth, chewing vigorously. "Wait." My feet froze in place. "I need to say goodbye first."

I stepped out from under the protective embrace and headed over to my first love. "Thank you, Ales, for last night. You have no idea what that means to me."

A small smile crept onto his face. "Maybe I do."

"You heading to Stavros' now?"

"I guess." He scuffed the boardwalk.

"Say hi to your family for me."

"Sure."

"Drive safe, will ya?"

"Always."

"Listen, about what was said last night…"

I wasn't sure I wanted to go there with Noah standing just a few feet away, but at the same time I couldn't just let Ales leave without knowing. "I've thought about what you asked me up there."

He narrowed his eyes just a touch and tipped his head to the side.

"Yes, I'll forgive you. I mean, I have already forgiven you. I'm no longer upset about… things." And it was the truth. My heart felt lighter and healed. Who knew it would take spending the night up on a mountain top to come to that conclusion?

"Thank you." His eyes glistened under the glare of the full sun. "That means a lot."

"Next time you're in town, will you call me? We'll go for Eggs Athabee."

"Of course."

"Great." I shifted the backpack on my shoulders. "Well, see you again sometime."

He bobbed his head and pulled off his toque. "Someday."

"Okay, bye." Something we never said to each other when he took off that day after I announced the sobering news of our creation. He'd just left. This time, there was a kind of finality to our goodbye.

I turned and walked back over to Noah, who lifted my back from my shoulders and carried it by the handle. We were just about at his car when Ales called out my name.

"Corrine, I forgot to give you my number."

"Right, and I forgot to send you that picture." I passed him my phone after unlocking it, and he sent himself a quick text. When I took it back, I sent him our selfie taken less than an hour ago, and yet, it felt like much longer.

"Thanks." He dropped his phone into his pocket.

"See ya."

Noah walked a few more feet and opened his truck door for me. "Hop in and warm up. There's some food for you." The sweetheart that he was, he brought a banana and a homemade sandwich, along with a steaming cup of something warm.

"Thank you, it's perfect."

I climbed inside and once Noah was in, he started it up and blasted the heat. Never again will I take heat for granted. It rolled over my feet and blew into my face, and I melted into the seat with a relaxed sigh. I chanced a glance out the window to see Ales, but he was gone. My heart contracted, but this time it didn't splinter open. That was that. It was over. We had a fabulous night together, cleared the air between and nothing more. There couldn't be a future. Even though we'd closed the gap between us, there was still too much physical distance. Worst part was, I'd seen my Ales up there, the one I'd fallen in love with all those years ago. He was still him and with that realisation, a new ache settled over me.

"So, how about a do over?"

"A what?" I whipped my head around.

Noah sat in the driver's seat; long legs folded under the dash. "We missed out on our planned date yesterday, on your birthday." He reached for my hand and caressed it. It didn't incite the same flutters and sensation as when Ales did it, but it was sweet all the same. "Let's redo it. How about tonight I pick you up and we'll drive into Hinton for a supper. I'll make reservations at that sushi place you like."

"Sure. That sounds nice." I tried to force a smile onto my face, but all I wanted was to go home. The heat was making me sleepy and a yawn bellowed out. I covered my mouth in haste. "Can we discuss the details later though? I'm rather tired."

"Didn't sleep that much?" There was a suspicious gaze as he stared at me and with it came the rise of his eyebrow.

"Kind of hard when there were no beds and we were sleeping on the floor, under a thin blanket." I straightened myself up and sunk into my jacket a bit. "I'm not feeling so fresh, and I'd just really like a hot shower and a wee nap. I think I'll feel human after that and will be ready to think clearly."

"Sure thing. Sorry for thinking something happened between you and that guy. How do you know him?"

"We went to high school together. Can you believe it? What are the odds that we'd run into each other after all this time? He's not even from around here, he's visiting from Victoria." My mouth ran on full and sped out the true details without giving away the full truth.

"That's pretty coincidental."

"Right? My psychic said I was going to have…" *Wait just a minute.*

"Sorry, what?" Noah gave me that same look everyone did whenever psychics were mentioned.

"It was a fun birthday gift to myself."

"You bought yourself a birthday gift?"

The hole I was digging was getting bigger by the minute. "Yes, sort of. My parents sent me cash for my birthday to spend on something I'd never get for myself, so I bought a reading with a psychic."

He covered the laugh he wanted to let fly. "Okay, I'll humour you because you haven't slept yet, and you were stranded up on a mountain for the night. What did your psychic claim would happen?"

"She said," I began, with a smart-assed expression on my face. "That I was going to have a monumental weekend, and that the power would shift altering my course. Of course, I knew I was going to have a great weekend, we were going out. Or will be tonight."

"And the power shifting?" His blond eyebrow was nearly as high as the upper summit boardwalk.

"Has to mean the tram station losing power, right?"

"See? Bullshit. They just take your money. Their predictions are garbage."

Maybe. But the power *had* shifted. And my course changed too. No longer was I weighed down with hurt and anger. There was some truth to my reading. Another yawn overcame me.

"Let's get you home. Do you want me to drive, or did you want to start your car and let it warm up?"

Hmm… the first option would mean I was committing to having him drive me back here at some point, where the second meant I could leave it open ended. I took in Noah's face, so sweet and handsome. Twenty-four hours ago, I'd been ready to give him all of me, and now there was hesitation. Why? It was Ales.

A future I no longer had but desperately craved. That wasn't fair. Not to Ales, who already vacated the parking lot. It wasn't fair to Noah, who was patient and kind and deserved someone to give her all to, but it wasn't fair to me. I'd been holding onto the past and over the course of the past twenty-four hours, had learned to let it go and live for the present and maybe, for once, a future.

"Can you drive me home?" I smiled over at him.

"With pleasure." He popped the truck into gear, and we drove away

Chapter
FOURTEEN

A few days had passed since the overnight stay on Whistler. Things with Noah had not progressed the way I anticipated and had planned before the tram ride. In fact, Noah drove me home and stayed with me for a bit, just long enough to finish breakfast together. Upon my insistence though, he left for a while but returned that night for our do-over.

Begrudgingly, I went but my heart wasn't into it and we ended the evening with a kiss, not the night cap we both had expected previously. With a heavy heart, I told him I needed time to think; about us, about me, and about what happened. A barrage of questions about Noah and I's relationship came to the surface, most of it wondering if I'd only been stringing him along or if deep down, I believed something good would come of it. Prior to that night on Whistler, I did have faith in the promise of more, but things shifted and changed, and it was all me. When probed again who Ales was, I told him the truth, without hesitation or remorse. My tear-filled monologue over, Noah stormed away, but not before grabbing the flowers he'd brought earlier.

Seriously, he was better off without me.

Today was my day off, and I needed a change of scenery from the shop and the walls of my home. I took my laptop downloaded with all the images of my overnight stay, and walked over to the café on Patricia Street, one of the main touristy roads in my quaint little town. I headed upstairs to the coffee shop overlooking the drag and grabbed a table outside. The air was chilly, but the shining sun attempted to warm me, and however cold it felt, it was still warmer than the upper summit had been.

A lovely male barista came over to my table with my freshly crafted drink and sat it beside my computer. "Sorry, I couldn't help but look. That's a gorgeous picture."

I'd been right, the picture of the sunrise with the mountain peak eclipsing part of it was stunning, and even more so on my computer screen rather than the tiny little screen of the camera.

"Thanks. I captured it up on Whistler."

He straightened himself up and stepped back, giving me a once over. "Wait a sec…"

"Yep, that was me." A full blush coloured my cheeks, turning them as red as my hair.

"You're like a local celebrity."

Which sadly, had become the case. However, it was small town gossip and soon something new would take its place because even though it happened a couple of days ago, I was tired of my fifteen minutes.

"Were you scared?"

"Not at all. In fact, it was rather enjoyable overall."

"Was it clear that night?"

Just remembering it brought a sweet smile to my face. "I've never seen the skies with so many stars."

"You're so lucky." He tucked his tray under his arm. "I've tried to book tickets for the Dark Sky festival event up there, but it always sells out. Did you get any pictures?"

I shook my head and crossed my legs as I leaned back in my chair. "I tried, but I didn't have a tripod."

"That super sucks."

I couldn't agree more. Oh well. Maybe I should try to get tickets for the festival. It didn't happen until October, but tickets for the events always went on sale early. I stared back at the screen.

The young man took his cue. "If you need anything else, please just flag me down."

"Thanks."

He walked back into the café and left me flipping through the photos. I stopped on the selfie of Ales and I, and I ran my finger down the screen, touching his face, wishing I could do it in real life.

"You're cute, you know."

I spun my head around so fast I was sure my chiropractor would have something to say about it. "Ales, what are you doing here?"

In his hands he held a take-away mug. "Desperately searching."

My heart pitter-pattered. "For what?" I knew this town like the back of my hand, and if someone wanted something specific, I knew exactly what store to direct them to.

"For you."

"Me?" My breath caught in my chest. It was too good to be true. "But how did you…?"

"Find you?" He chuckled as he set down his drink. "You're not hard to miss. I was wandering the street on that side, and I stopped to pose with that bear."

I laughed, knowing exactly what bear he was referring to. Jasper the Bear was a touristy gimmick, and people always seemed to stop and take pictures with the painted concrete statue, especially the one in front of the sweets shop.

"And frustrated in not being able to find the shop you work in, I happened to look up here. There you were."

"Divine intervention?"

"Maybe." He took a lingering sip.

"I still don't understand why though." I wanted to believe he'd come back to continue what we started, but that was too good to be true. Miracles like that never happened, especially to me.

"You see, I left you once, and it damn near killed us both. I can't do it again." He set his drink down on the table and pulled a chair over. "When I talked to Stavros, who says hi by the way, he said I was given a gift, something I can't deny. It was too coincidental to have been up on the mountain, and then to see you there." He wrapped his warm hands around mine. "After everything we said, I'd be a fool to pass up another chance with you." A low throat clearing sound filled the space between us. "I'm here to ask you to pick me, not Noah."

A smile bubbled out of me as a million thoughts swirled in my head. "You're in luck. Noah and I weren't an exclusive item. I told him about us, about that night, and he stormed away." The memory of the pained expression on Noah's face made me shudder. "He's a super sweet guy."

Ales hung his head ever so slightly and lowered his voice. "Would you rather him?"

I shook my head and stared at our tangled hands. "I couldn't be with him knowing how I still feel about you." My heart raced at the endless possibilities of where this conversation was headed.

"And? How is that?"

I shrugged and released my breath, taking in the sparkle in his eye and the gentle smile threatening to expand from cheek to cheek. "I still love you. Over the years that never went away. Ever."

That beautiful grin widened fully. "Me either. It's always been you."

My heart skipped a beat. "So now what? How do we move forward?"

"We'll find a way. Obviously, it's meant to be, right? But we can start with facetime and daily calls, like we used to, and progress to where we'll live. I can't make you move to Sooke, and I'm not sure I want to move here considering my marine biology career would go belly up in a town where the nearest ocean is fourteen hours away."

Total truth. Of the two of us, I was the one who had more flexibility in careers, being that I didn't have one to speak of. I worked in retail, but I could do that anywhere. Could I give up my sweet little mountain town for love? I wasn't sure, but for love, for Ales, I was going to try. Somehow though, I had a feeling, this time it was forever.

Epilogue

"Are you ready?"

In all my life, I had never been more ready for anything. I nodded at my dad who stood radiant in his silver suit. The rest of my family were already standing around the boardwalk, waiting for Dad and me to exit the observation area.

Originally, my parents weren't on board with the idea of Ales and I getting married at the top of Whistler's Mountain, but they hadn't been truly thrilled with the two of us getting back together either. However, they relented, eventually, and welcomed him into the family.

Ales and I packed up my small-town life in Jasper and moved to the island, a few months after reconciling. I got a job at a local bookstore, and inspired by the travel section, put together one of my own.

My first publication was a memoir about the night we were trapped on the summit, complete with photographs. I'd love to say it was a huge blockbuster, but I'm sure to the big authors, it wasn't what you'd call a success. To me, though, it became a best seller in its category and the town of Jasper has copies in just about every little shop on the main drag. It may have slightly elevated my celebrity status.

I stood in the observation area, giving the downstairs space a heavy visual sweep. The tables and chairs were the same as they had been a couple of years ago, and the gift shop had remained untouched. On the shelf near the register in the gift shop, I spotted a couple of copies of my book. I'd have to check the numbers, but I was pretty sure the summit gift shop was my best retailer.

Above me, chairs moved around in preparation for the thirty guests for our reception in the not-so-newly-renovated kitchen and restaurant area. The one not quite ready for guests when the power stopped two fateful years ago.

And speaking of power, the gentle hum of the tram house rumbled beneath my feet. Since that night, the generator had been upgraded, although the source of the power failure had never been solved. The station had remained vacant for three days following our rescue, and just as suddenly as the power vanished, it returned.

It was a glorious spring afternoon. The weather had cooperated enough that the entire summit was snow free, giving our guests the opportunity to walk up the trails to the peak. Most of the guests were in suits and cocktail dresses, so it was debatable if they would or not. I certainly wouldn't be traversing the trails, not in my fancy wedding dress, even if I was wearing runners instead of high heels.

"Whenever you're ready," Tony spoke again, peeking his head outside and popping it back in again. "Everyone's good to go."

I looped my hand through my father's, and we headed outside, after first smiling at Tony.

The wind was breezy, just enough to make my veil float in the air. We walked down the boardwalk filled only with the hushed voices of the invited guests. I slowly, but eagerly, made my way to the end where my darling husband-to-be – Alessandro – stood waiting in his black tuxedo in front of the Justice of the Peace.

Dad stopped at the edge of the wooden walkway and shook Ales' hand, before putting my hand into my future.

"You look gorgeous." Ales linked his hand through mine.

"As do you."

He winked and together we walked the last few steps to the waiting officiant.

We were getting married, the happiest day of my life so far, and I'd had several since our reconciliation. My attitude on the future had changed, and my future was as bright as the sunlight shining down on all of us. Life was grand.

I turned to glance at the people in the front. My sister with her husband and their children, and my dad standing beside my mom who was holding our eight-week old son.

Life was pretty damn amazing.

I gave Ales' hand a squeeze and turned to

face the man of my dreams.

The Justice of the Peace cleared his throat and began. "Dearly Beloved..."

Dear Reader

How was that? Did you enjoy? Share what you liked, what you loved, or even what you hated. I'd love to hear from you via email, my website, or a review on your favourite retailer site. It doesn't have to be long, even just as simple as "Enjoyed the chemistry" works. Reviews and ratings help me gain visibility, and as I'm sure you can tell from my books, reviews are tough to come by. If you have the time for an extra review, here's my author page on Goodreads .

If you would like to be kept abreast of when I'm releasing the next story, be sure to join my mailing list. I promise not to spam you (they come every two weeks) and I keep things brief with lots of freebies. Your time is valuable, and I appreciate how you've spent time reading my story (thank you for that!). I share behind the scenes information, do a paperback giveaway every so often, and even send you on an easy scavenger hunt for a free book.

As an author, it makes my day when a reader or blogger share their thoughts and gives me feedback on the characters they've invested their time in. When readers fall in love with a character, it's encouraging to write more. Fun fact, when I finished writing *Duly Noted* and released it, a lot of readers wanted to know more about the friendship between Lucas and Aurora, and because of those emails, *That Summer* came to be. Thank you so much for spending time with me.

Yours,

H.M. Shander

Others To Read

Add these reads to your collection.

Run Away Charlotte
Ask Me Again
Duly Noted
That Summer
If You Say Yes
Serving Up Innocence
Serving Up Devotion
Serving Up Secrecy
Serving Up Hope
It All Began with a Note
It All Began with a Mai-Tai
It All Began with a Wedding
Noel
Whistler's Night

Coming SOON
Unmasking River (A Lover's Masquerade)
Return to Cheshire Bay
Adrift in Cheshire Bay
Awake in Cheshire Bay
Guarding Her Heart (Game Changer boxed set)
Christmas in Cheshire Bay (Sugar Plum Kisses)

Thank yous

I am in awe that this is my fourteenth published novel! Number FOURTEEN! Holy smokes. They say writing is a solo endeavor (most of the time), but I know I couldn't be where I am without the support of many people, starting with...

My Shander family, whom you may know on my social media platforms as Hubs, The Teen, and Little Dude. Thank you from the bottom of my heart for letting me pursue what I love doing, for something that allows me to transport myself to another time and place. Thank you for cheerleading and encouraging me to keep going and to chase my dreams, and for the nonstop coffees I sometimes needed when I was on a role. I love you all with my whole heart.

To my parents, in-laws and extended family – Thank you for your endless support and encouraging your friends and family to give my books a try. Having you visit me at markets and book signings means the world. I have an amazing family, and everyday I'm thankful to you all. Thanks for being you.

To my wonderfully dedicated alpha reader – Mandy. Gosh, girl. You and I have been at this almost since day one, but I can't think of another who is my go-to gal, the one who pulls out the tough love when needed and yet is the first in line to congratulate me. You see the story, in its rawest state, and point out the diamond hidden within. You let me know when the story is fantastic, or whether that chapter needs more work (and it always does!) I trust in your words. This is a hard world, and yet, we've become amazing friends and comrades, and I'm so very grateful for our growing friendship. One day, we're going to meet up. Just not sure what side of the border it will be.

To my beta reader – Josephine. Every email from you is a gift. You highlight what works, what so does not, and even tell me to chop all the cheesy/cliché lines and make the story better. Your dedication to the strength of my words is powerful and because of your insight and willingness to review the chapter over and over until it is perfect, it nothing short of awe inspiring. I'm so thrilled your novels are starting to make traction, and I wish nothing but the best for you!

To my cover designer – Francessca. When I saw this cover, I knew I needed it. I knew the perfect story for it and now the two have finally merged. I look forward to having you create another cover, and I've noticed many other illustrated premades on your website... Hmm... which one to grab first?

To my editor – Irina. Thanks for your dedication to fixing my errors and highlighting the inconsistencies. I truly hope I am getting better at this, as the old mistakes don't seem to be happening as much anymore. Now, there are all brand new ones! LOL. At least I'm keeping us both on our toes.

If I missed you, it certainly wasn't intentional. I know I couldn't be where I am without the help of so many others. Thank you! And thank you for reading and making it all the way to the end. You all rock.

About the Author

H.M. Shander knows four languages—English, French, Sarcasm and ASL—and speaks two of them exceptionally well. Any guesses which two? She lives in beautiful Edmonton, AB, a big city with a small-town feel; where all her family live within a twenty-minute drive, although her parents are contemplating moving away. As much as she would love the beach under a blanket of stars, this is her home.

A big-time coffee addict, she prefers to start her day with a mug before attending to anything pressing, like driving the #momtaxi as she shuttles her kids off to school and various extracurricular activities. Secretly she loves it as when the vehicle is empty, it gives her time to think about what crazy things those characters will do next (need something to kill the drive time LOL). She is a self-proclaimed science nerd (and friends/family will back this up), however, likes to be creative when there's time. Right brain, left brain? Both.

No matter how many different jobs she's worked, her favourite has been working as a birth doula and librarian, in addition to being a romance author. Because, let's be honest, who doesn't love falling in love?

You can follow her on Facebook, Twitter and Goodreads.

Thanks for reading– all the way to the very end.

Manufactured by Amazon.ca
Bolton, ON

38215943R00081